THE
OCCIDENTAL HOTEL

Essential Prose Series 181

 Canada Council   Conseil des Arts
for the Arts   du Canada

 ONTARIO ARTS COUNCIL
CONSEIL DES ARTS DE L'ONTARIO

an Ontario government agency
un organisme du gouvernement de l'Ontario

Canadä

Guernica Editions Inc. acknowledges the support of the Canada Council
for the Arts and the Ontario Arts Council. The Ontario Arts Council
is an agency of the Government of Ontario.

We acknowledge the financial support of the Government of Canada.

THE
OCCIDENTAL HOTEL

John Bentley Mays

With Essays By
Antanas Sileika,
Anne Collins &
Richard Rhodes

**GUERNICA
EDITIONS**
TORONTO • CHICAGO
BUFFALO • LANCASTER (U.K.)
2020

Michael Mirolla, editor
David Moratto, interior and cover design
Cover Image: *Portrait of John Bentley Mays* By Gertrude Kearns
Interior images: © Estate of Joseph Beuys / SOCAN (2019)
Guernica Editions Inc.
287 Templemead Drive Hamilton, (ON), Canada L8W 2W4
2250 Military Road, Tonawanda, N.Y. 14150-6000 U.S.A.
www.guernicaeditions.com

Distributors:
Independent Publishers Group (IPG)
600 North Pulaski Road, Chicago IL 60624
University of Toronto Press Distribution,
5201 Dufferin Street, Toronto (ON), Canada M3H 5T8
Gazelle Book Services, White Cross Mills
High Town, Lancaster LA1 4XS U.K.

First edition.
Printed in Canada.

Legal Deposit—Third Quarter
Library of Congress Catalog Card Number: 2019949188
Library and Archives Canada Cataloguing in Publication
Title: The occidental hotel / John Bentley Mays with essays by Antanas Sileika,
Anne Collins & Richard Rhodes.
Names: Mays, John Bentley, author.
Description: Series statement: Essential prose series ; 181
Identifiers: Canadiana (print) 2019017479X | Canadiana (ebook) 20190174846
| ISBN 9781771835145 (softcover) | ISBN 9781771835152 (EPUB)
| ISBN 9781771835169 (Kindle)
Classification: LCC PS8576.A92 O23 2020 | DDC C813/.54—dc23

THE
OCCIDENTAL HOTEL

ABOUT THIS NOVEL
AND THE MAN WHO WROTE IT

Antanas Sileika

John Bentley Mays wore shapeless sweat pants and a baggy sweater when he walked into Little Italy's Bar Diplomatico to meet me. He was unshaven and since he wasn't wearing a hat, the prominent scar on his forehead where skin cancers had been cut out repeatedly made him look like a war vet of some kind. He was there yet again to discuss with me the progress of the novel you hold in your hands.

This version of John was a far cry from the dapper Truman Capote knock-off I'd met along with his writer wife, Margaret Cannon, in the early eighties, when John was a sizzling *Globe and Mail* critic who made Canadian art essential and important enough to fight about. He could be scornful of sacred cows and worked hard to elevate young artists. A brilliant conversationalist when in good form, he could take a conceit and spin it into a talk worthy of an essay. His writing was a delight to read, full of unexpected turns and insights.

For much more on John the man, the critic and the intellectual, see the essays by Anne Collins and Rick Rhodes that follow at the end of this book.

First evangelical, then Anglican, then Catholic, first an alcoholic and then a teetotaller, first art and then culture and architecture critic, he had had his share of ups and downs.

A lifelong depressive, he'd been fed a variety of drugs and gone through a variety of treatments including electroshock therapy, and all of these seemed to work for a while and then failed him. Among the things he carried was a fraught Louisiana childhood—a murdered father and a mother who died young so John was shipped off to older sisters when he was a child. He left behind his southern gothic background to come north where art and Toronto and his wife, Margaret, were his antidotes to an unhappy childhood worthy of William Faulkner.

The one quality he had was an ability to write though the pain, and now he was writing a novel. We met repeatedly at the Dip to discuss the first fifty pages, then the first hundred pages, and then the first one hundred and fifty pages all the way from 2013 through to 2016. John always rewrote from the beginning and continued to the current end, so I must have read parts of this novel six or seven times.

I was shocked and appalled, admiring and afraid for his reputation as John wrote an unconventional piece of work with one of the most horrible anti-hero narrators I had read since John Fowles' *The Collector*. And there is no escape from this monster, who suffers no comeuppance, and who, like a poisonous spider, sits in a web with different threads: elements of art criticism; ironic comments on modernity; outlandish pulp adventures worthy of Edgar Rice Burroughs; mood pieces like those of W G Sebald; and explorations of Nazi youth ideology as it affected the late German artist Joseph Beuys (1921-1986).

John was fascinated by Joseph Beuys, and one of the unconventional aspects of this novel is that it contains images from some of this artist's performance pieces. The stand-in for Beuys in the novel is a character named Jupp, someone John uses to explore in a fictional way Beuys' own Nazi youth. Beuys had been a Luftwaffe pilot during the Second World War, and later biographies accused him of having been not only a soldier, but a true Nazi. John both admired Beuys and was deeply troubled by this past. John held his dismay and esteem for Beuys in some kind of tension in his mind.

The fictional Jupp is an object of fascination for the narrator of this novel, a murderous, racist southerner holed up in a crumbling hotel called The Occidental Hotel, a place that is a shell of the American postwar optimism during which it was built. Modernity was a lifelong obsession for John, primarily through its expression in architecture.

Some form of modernity was going to free John from his biography of gothic southern history, but it never managed to do so. John wrestled with these two elements for his entire life, dealing with these themes and many others in some of his nonfiction books such as *Power in the Blood* and *Arrivals*.

The narrator also has a half brother who sets off to seek redemption and insight in some kind of tawdry version of James Hilton's *Lost Horizon*, in which the answer to life's mysteries are held in a remote Himalayan lamasery.

I cautioned John that many Canadian readers would hate this book because it provides no exit. We see various depictions of hell with little solace or redemption. I warned him that he would be confused with the narrator of this book, and he told me the narrator was the man he would have become had he stayed in the south. John said he had no intention of shocking Canadians. He wanted to reprimand Americans, especially after the horror of the 2015 Charleston Church massacre, in which a white supremacist shot and killed nine black parishioners in a church and wounded three others.

For three years we talked about this novel. I suggested that John was dealing in arcana because hardly anyone outside the art world knows who Joseph Beuys was. I accused him of delivering a bleak vision, and he agreed that he was working in the realm of dark romanticism, but could not give up his obsessions. I was fascinated by this work, which felt decidedly European to me, like nothing else I was seeing in Canada. I have mentioned W G Sebald, but I might add Cees Nooteboom as a comparison, two writers who observed civilization with melancholy eyes.

On September 2, 2016, John sent me the final draft of his novel. It was highly polished, as all of John's work tended to be, but I don't think it was perfect. I suggested he make a few changes to speed up the action in the first part of the novel, and he seemed to agree with my ideas. We made arrangements to meet again at the Dip on September 21 to discuss my notes. On September 16, he died of a massive heart attack after walking up a hill in High Park with his long-time friend, the literary critic, Phil Marchand.

A manuscript by a deceased writer is a hard sell, but Guernica

Editions agreed with me that this novel is an important addition to Canadian letters for at least two reasons. First, it is an unblinking look into a heart of darkness of a kind we almost never see in this country. It is frightening and necessary. And second, it is the final document of a razor-sharp mind that helped form Canadian culture over several decades.

Antanas Sileika is a Toronto novelist.

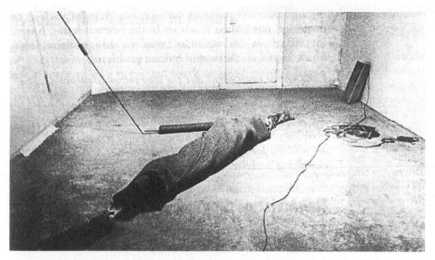

Figure 1: A photograph taken during the Action entitled *The Chief-Fluxus Chant*, which occurred at the René Block Gallery, Berlin, on 1 December 1964. The German artist Joseph Beuys, shrouded in felt, was stretched out on the floor of a small white room. Dead hares were placed at his head and feet. A microphone carried his sounds to loudspeakers.

It is said that these sounds were: "[H]eartbeats, his respiration, wheezing, coughing, sighing, grumbling, hissing, whistling, and his pronunciation of mumbled letters of the alphabet." (Lucrezia De Domizio Durini, trans. Howard Rodger MacLean, The Felt Hat: Joseph Beuys, A Life Told *[Milano: Edizioni Charta, 1997], page 30.)*

Joseph Beuys is reported (in Durini, page 31) to have said: "… my presence inside the felt … was a parallel to the old initiation rite of the coffin, a form of simulated death. It takes a great deal of discipline to avoid panic in such conditions—acting out being dead, empty, emotionless, without specific sensations of claustrophobia and pain, for nine hours in the same position … In a certain sense, it's a death, a real action and not just an interpretation."

In a story from the early 1880s, Mark Twain describes a Munich establishment in which the bodies of the recently deceased were monitored for signs of revival. Each corpse was provided with a finger ring attached by a wire to a bell, so that, by a very small movement, the body could make its vitality known to an attendant at once. Such hostels for the presumed (but not certainly) dead existed in several other German cities well into the twentieth century, their existence prompted by the worry of families that their officially defunct loved ones might actually be not quite dead, after all. Distrust of death certificates, a symptom of the more general, growing suspicion of the absolutist state and hierarchical Church, was widespread in Europe following the publication, in 1749, of Jean-Jacques Bruhier's immensely popular Dissertation sur l'incertitude des signes de la mort et l'abus des enterremens & embaumemens précipités. *Ancient wisdom held that, once a person's wheezing, coughing, sighing, grumbling, hissing, whistling had ceased, the person could be considered definitely dead. This certainty, crucial to the relatives' peace of mind, was overthrown by Bruhier's book.*

The Enlightenment squelched the Christian hope embodied in the doctrine of the Resurrection of the Body at the end of history, and introduced the fearful possibility of another, now horrible destiny. In this new scenario, the unexpectedly reviving body could find itself unable to escape shroud and coffin, condemned to die (finally, this time) of suffocation and terror, and starkly bereft of sacramental or familial consolation. Anxiety about (and fascination with) Scheintod persisted from Bruhier's time until embalming and cremation became common practices among Christians. It may have remained entrenched longer, and not only in Germany. According to legend, almost certainly spurious, a telephone was installed in the Cambridge, Massachusetts, sepulchre of Mary Baker Eddy, founder of the Church of Christ, Scientist, when she was laid to rest there, in 1910.

Like all other works by Beuys, The Chief-Fluxus Chant *seemed to have come from high antiquity or, even earlier, in the* Urzeit *of the human race. The performance was "a death, a real action" — and it recalls a particular kind of death, being buried alive, that haunted European imagination for nearly 200 years.*

The shaman, whose character Beuys attempted to imitate and assimilate, also undergoes Scheintod, also emits strange noises when immersed in a trance state. Reporting on a shamanic séance in his A

New Voyage and Description of the Isthmus of America *(1699), the explorer Lionel Wafer notes that the conjurers "continued some time at their Exercise, and we could hear them make most hideous Yellings and Shrieks; imitating the Voices of all their kind of Birds and Beasts."* Robert Burton, in The Anatomy of Melancholy *(1621), following the prejudice of his age, dismisses shamans as charlatans, but impressive ones: "They can counterfeit the voices of all birds and brute beasts almost, all tones and tunes of men, and speak within their throats, as if they spoke afar off, that they make their auditors believe they hear spirits, and are thence much astonished and affrighted with it."*

1

The strange mid-winter weather in Düsseldorf, in the municipal district of Heerdt, where this takes place on a day in early 1956, has nothing to do with what happens. It might do so, were Jupp to notice how unnaturally dry the air is today, how it lingers, windlessly, bright and unstirring, around the dormers and angles of the elderly house his studio is in, which he does not. The weather might play a part in this narrative, were it to tempt Jupp to go outdoors, which it does not.

Drawn from inside by the afternoon's unseasonable radiance, winter-pale tenants in the apartment block next door, the property managed by Götz, who also superintends Jupp's house, visit on the sidewalk beside the sunny brick and plastered walls that line the narrow street. Some of those on the sidewalk say that many more days like this and the buds will be tricked into opening early. One says the birds that came from Lapland last autumn will be perplexed.

Two men in their forties, each like Jupp a veteran of the eastern front, argue about an item that has been in the news, though not recently. They are loud, but I cannot make out what they say, their accents disorient my ear, which is tuned to the standard dialect of German I learned from listening to records. But now I think I understand — the topic is rearmament, I'm sure of it — though why they are going back and forth about this old news now, after the matter has been resolved as the weapons manufacturers and the Americans wanted, I do not

9

know. Why the men occasionally stab the still afternoon air with their fingers to drive home a point, I also do not know. Because I do not know, I can tell Alexander nothing about the matter.

An emaciated teenaged girl, who believes in nothing, has painted herself with American cosmetics so bright that she fluoresces like neon tubing. She listens to a ponderous Motorola portable radio, turned up loud, tuned to the American Forces Network, which is playing an Elvis song, just released. She stops listening to the melody for a moment, and says something I cannot make out to a husky blond youth who may or may not be her boyfriend, but is certainly not her brother. While listening to her, he throws his yo-yo toward the sidewalk, where he walks-the-dog on the pavement for a few instants before reeling in the toy, which has been manufactured in Luck, Wisconsin. The fabric for his shirt came off a factory loom at Spartanburg, South Carolina. His Jockey briefs are said by advertisements in magazines for young men to provide better support than boxer shorts, and the youth believes this to be true, because he feels, or thinks he feels, better support. He believes almost nothing else to be true. Begotten during his father's last leave before Stalingrad, where the father died, the blond son was hardly more than a toddler in 1945, when the idea of National Socialism was consigned to the cellar into which victors always put the visions of the defeated. So the youth with the yo-yo grew up without that idea, but without any other idea, and now believes nothing.

A woman with a podgy bosom, but without a waist, dressed in a leatheroid trench coat two sizes too small for her — she is surely not yet forty — smokes a cigarette in public, like an American. It is 1956, so she believes nothing. She believed something — it — everything — in 1937. Agape with awe and gratitude then, she hailed what she believed with a stiffly erect right arm, when the midnight-blue, open-topped Mercedes Benz 770K bearing it heaved slowly forward on the street between police lines, and burghers and little girls and she herself acclaimed it. Then came the bombs, and what she believed disappeared into the bunker beneath the Reich Chancellery in Berlin, where it shot itself in the spring of 1945, after which date she believed nothing at all. In 1956, she thinks about the television set and other appliances she does not yet own, she washes her husband's underwear with efficient detergents, everything is white and clean when she is done. There is nothing more to be said about her.

The Federal Republic of Germany is a normal country in Europe, one veteran of the eastern front says to the other, who replies it is not. Ten years have gone by since the Third Reich went under, so it's time, or it is not. Adenauer did not believe in German rearmament, then he did. Now there is the menace of Russia, always that, or there is not, but some things never change, and Russia is one of them. The shorter of the two men, who lost toes to frostbite when the German army's advance stalled before Moscow, is sure of it. The other man, standing with arms akimbo, says he saw something in a newsreel that convinced him otherwise, though he cannot say what it was, or why. (I dutifully cite the dialogue, so that Alexander will know what it means to be alive in 1956.)

The woman in the leatheroid coat interrupts the exchange of the two men to say that her husband will buy a television set if movies do not improve. I had intended to ignore her, but I cannot, because she wants a television set and says so. I am certain about this, since it is 1956 in West Germany, the citizens of which, by and large, want television sets. She also wants the body of the projectionist, aged 23, who lives with his sister three doors down the hallway, who, she imagines wrongly, shoots dice with girls for money and kisses in the projection booth while the feature ratchets through the sprockets, who told the woman in the leatheroid coat that German movies are bad and getting worse, but the American ones are the worst of all. She may have him some day, only if her husband dies or loses his mind, because she can fantasize about adultery, but cannot, owing to religious prejudices that have survived the loss of all sense of the transcendent, bring herself to plan it.

Upon hearing the woman's complaint about the movies, the man without some toes asks: What is wrong with the movies? I don't think they are so bad, especially the German ones about life in the countryside, maybe in the Alps or the Black Forest, like films before the war. There was one, I guess it was last year, about a farm girl who is seduced by a fancy man and goes with him to the city, but who comes home, broken-hearted, and is romanced out of her miseries and city ways by the farmer's son, whom she marries. That was a good one, with the kind of ending I like nowadays. The scenes of the mountain valley the farm was in were outstanding, so what could be bad about that? I don't like American movies, except for westerns.

I hear the woman start to explain her position on the movies, why she should have a television set. The youth is no longer hurling his yo-yo to within an inch of the pavement, then walking-the-dog. The girl listens to the radio.

Jupp, too, hears the voices and sounds rising from the sidewalk outside his studio's window, but he (unlike me) does not attend to what they mean. I want to know what they are saying, so I can tell Alexander they believe in nothing. Jupp could go out. No physical impediment prevents him from leaving the studio in the decayed house built in another century, nothing material stops him from joining the neighbours who stand on the sidewalk, talking and listening to each other talking, or listening to the radio. Nothing in his body stops him from strolling slowly and alone, as he does from time to time when the weather is clement, along Am Hochhofen beside the Erftkanal, or by the row of whitewashed, buxom houses that front onto Rheinallee and the river beyond. He is not curious this afternoon about what is spoken by the people outside his window, or about anything else that transpires in Heerdt, where the tenants from next door talk in the warm air about rearmament and the movies, or about nothing. He does not care to know why his house, alone on its street, escaped destruction by the bombs.

The box was delivered an hour ago.

2

His eyes and fingertips play over the surface of the box, scanning it for flaws. The box, he concludes after a few minutes of looking and feeling, has come as specified from the joinery in his home-town of Kleve, a small conurbation that mantles the slopes of a prominence crowned by a castle, the Schwanenberg, in the Lower Rhineland, very near Holland, which is flatter. The box actually existed in 1956, within a time continuous with the history that you and I inhabit, that Jupp inhabited, 1921–1986. These facts, Jupp's dates and the existence and use of the box, are recorded in the vindictive biography, which I despise, which Alexander would despise, were he to read anything other than what I write, and the novels of Edgar Rice Burroughs. The box's corners are held tightly together by brass clamps. The hardwood planking has been sanded smooth, and the exterior of the box has been lightly slathered with black tar. The side that swings open has been fastened to the frame with butterfly hinges and furnished with a hook-and-eye latch on the inside.

I have a snapshot of Jupp, nude except for swimming trunks, taken at a sunny Italian beach in 1960, when he was 39 years old, before his logic-jamming rituals, mystery plays, his sculptures, his widely reported confrontations, made him known to avant-gardists, the respectable, the police, the bemused readers of newspapers. The figure in the photo has the body of a blacksmith, or that of some other man who labours with

13

his hands — a body neither slim and springy nor heavy and fleshy, not honed by systematic exercise or military rigour, but natively stolid and broad-beamed and wide in the chest. The flesh of his arms is knit to long bones ending in sizeable hands that could have once been accustomed to the heft of hammers, but were not. He has big feet. Judging from the near-naked body in the picture, I suspect that certain women found him physically attractive, though not fascinating, when he was 39 — women of a robust nature, that is, who wanted their men framed by strong bones clad in flat muscles, and free from every trace of the epicene, the neurotic and submissive, as men should be.

He is bare-headed in the photograph, which makes the image a rarity. It is historical fact, to which thousands of pictures bear witness, that, from around 1956, he wore a hat in public, a homburg of English origin, but he does not do so here, because he has not yet emerged from his crisis and assumed a conspicuous role in German culture. Before he started wearing the hat, he let his lank hair grow long on the sides, then combed the limp fringe up and over his pate in an attempt to hide impending baldness, which worried him, would always bother him. Then he started wearing the hat. Other theories have been put forward to explain the near-omnipresent hat. Critics have argued that the homburg was ceremonial regalia, a crown or headdress of the sort worn by priests or the Lords of Misrule, something that asserted his status as shaman, spiritual healer, a dispenser of impropriety, irrationality, to those oppressed by liberal reason's pieties and conventional morality. The same critics usually maintain that the hat's material fabric, felt, is significant, given the notorious public persona he cultivated after 1956 — certain felts being composed of the fulled, compressed fur of rabbits, which have been held by some primordial story-tellers (according to modern ethnographers) to be sacredly prolific, tricksterish, pranksterish, paradoxical, perversely creative, all rabbits being sexually wanton. Such speculations do not interest me.

I prefer facts, such as another photograph I possess, this one presumably taken by his friend Nylons, which matters to me now. According to information inscribed in pencil on the back, *January–1956*, it was snapped in the studio after he had stopped eating. He stands, bare-headed, trousered, shirted, booted, by his bed. Why he permitted himself to be photographed when he had become gaunt, I cannot say. Were I to stop eating, I would care enough about my appearance to forestall any bid to photograph me — or so I think, but cannot know, since I cannot imagine fasting, even while grieving, as he was grieving in this period. The quasi-monastic Christian rule according to which Sister lives requires her to fast on Fridays and during Lent, but I suspect she fasts at other times to spite me, since she knows I disdain fasting and other religious practices.

Jupp's skull gives the face the shape of a death's head. Cheek-knobs jut out below sunken indigo eyes that communicate no inwardness, no luminous thought. They are as free from shine as the undersides of clouds before rain, like the eyes one sees in daguerreotypes of Confederate soldiers whose heads are clamped in place for the long exposure, or pictures of Hitler Youth cadres at attention, or being reviewed, their faces and bodies emptied of subjectivity, idiosyncrasy, of all moral movement except obedience. The viewer's eye is drawn to the mouth, sensuous, full-lipped, even faintly negroid (or so Alexander thinks, incorrectly), and slightly too ample for the spade-shaped prow of his jaw. The tint of his skin is that of a well-known European racial subset, the Teutonic. The box is big enough for a man his size to sit inside.

He runs his hand over the side of the box, and is silent. Among the other artists whose company he kept before Christmas, 1955, when he stopped going out, Jupp has not been famous as a conversationalist. His familiar utterances to his friends have been quiet, almost shy monologues about a strange stillness, a tedious calm in his mind. He has wanted to be an artist, but lately has had trouble thinking of what to make or draw. He could be an artist, he said, because he had been the outstanding student in his class at Düsseldorf's academy. Yet, since Christmas, he has made nothing. Friends listened to him in the summer and autumn of 1955, when he was engaged to the woman who works in the post office, and then ceased to listen.

Nylons, who will abduct Jupp later tonight, was one who did listen, and who still does, in early 1956. A week ago, when Nylons dropped off cigarettes, food and beer at the studio, Jupp told Nylons that he had ordered from Kleve a box big enough to sit inside, where he intended to hide himself on winter afternoons and nights, listen to nothing outside his body, think about nowhere, though he might think of places utterly elsewhere, like Tibet, where holy men lived and the air was thin and pure. Nylons sat on the edge of the huge nuptial bed in the studio, and he listened to Jupp, who stood stark still, as he would when the second photograph I have was taken, though in the middle of the room, beside his drawing table, his long hands tightened into fists.

3

Jupp told Nylons about a dawn in June, 1945, when he, Jupp, foraged for food on the marshy margins of the British prisoner-of-war compound at Cuxhaven, in northwestern Germany. Jupp was actually taken to a camp at Cuxhaven after his paratrooper unit surrendered in the last days of the war. This fact is in the biography. It is probably true that he and the other exhausted inmates were hungry. I have invented the statement that some prisoners had eaten grass and made themselves sicker than they already were, though something like that could have taken place, since German prisoners starved in the camps.

He thought he could help his fellow-prisoners by remembering which wild plants were edible and which were not. He had learned to make this discrimination in 1936-1937, when he walked abroad in the forests, across the pastures around Kleve, on the edges of ploughed fields. In circumstances I will describe later, he had learned, from manuals and wildlife guides he discovered in an unfrequented corner of the town library, the names and potencies of many plants growing wild in the district.

But that June morning in 1945, he could not recall which plants were edible ones. The knowledge had pleased him, delighted him even; and now it failed to answer the call back from whatever dingy, forsaken laneway of the mind it had disappeared into. He had known want since the war began; he had been hungry during his hasty evacuation from

Crimea before advancing Soviet armies, had suffered injury to his head, to his leg. He was weary, sick, hungry above all, but this forgetting, this vaporing away of certain memories pained him more than the hunger.

You became a model prisoner, Nylons said. You did not steal food from the other inmates in the camp, you did not sodomize other prisoners, you did not join those whom the British called incorrigibles, who wanted it to go on and on, after the surrender, even in the camps, where there was no point to it any longer. You were very tired, so you forgot everything that had pleased you then, before the war, during it, without being forced to do so. You allowed the wrecked streets and city squares of your mind to be swept clean of thoughts of former pleasure that could have troubled you in the new Germany that the British captors released you into, in August, 1945.

Jupp said that, during the first morning's walk out of Cuxhaven, he found an abandoned bicycle. He wheeled into Kleve just before sunset a couple of days after he had set out, steered the bike among the piles of blackened masonry and timbers on Tiergartenstrasse, where he had lived with his parents before the war, and to which his elders returned after their newer place was bombed. The stairwell and corridor that led him to his parents' apartment stank of garbage, old men, and the sour stench of fires, now exhausted, that had wasted other houses in the neighbourhood after the bombers flew away, but not this one.

Jupp told Nylons that, in the late summer of his home-coming to Kleve, he hunted for love in a street where he had heard or imagined he could find it. The destination was the cellar of a building partially destroyed, in a laneway bordered by tall, empty-eyed façades pawing the night sky. The cellar's yellow light spilled out of the low door into the street. A rotund man named Fleischer, formerly the proprietor of a ladies' wear emporium where Jupp's mother shopped, before and after it was Aryanized, had improvised a bar in the cellar of his ruined store, furnished it with injured but serviceable chairs and tables pulled from the wreckage, arranged for it to be supplied with black-market gin, which the patrons paid for in cigarettes.

Drinking slowly and silently at the tables, while Fleischer wiped the counter that did not need wiping and smoked a stump of cigar, ex-soldiers were hunched over glasses. Anyone could tell they had been soldiers, since they were young. Jupp had believed women would be there. The men in the makeshift bar looked at him.

Where are the women? Jupp asked Fleischer. Some were around, Fleischer whispered, but they went to wherever the GIs are. Didn't want to go with German men. I told them this would be a good place to work. They went anyway. I guess I was wrong.

During his summer in the prisoner of war camp at Cuxhaven, Jupp told Nylons, he had known soldiers without battles to fight and without women gather themselves into cliques of three or four, choose brides from among the younger inmates, who were rewarded for love and absolute obedience with food, cigarettes, protection. Jupp had been neither a master nor a bride. The men drinking in the bar were not harsh and urgent, as the masters among the prisoners had been.

They watched me, unspeaking, Jupp told Nylons, when I slipped out the door into the darkness and rubble lit by the papery yellow light of the bar. They forgot something in the camp, too, he said, they forgot the bodies of women that pleased them before the end. I never forgot that, Jupp said, just everything else, or something else. Gone were pictures and pleasures, things my body had felt, remembered, before I stopped remembering which plants were edible, in June, 1945.

You became a model prisoner, Nylons said, you forgot, you ceased to have inappropriate, half-waking dreams prompted by boyhood readings from the *Prose Edda,* by the eclectic, post-Christian theorizing of Rudolf Steiner about bees, their society and sacred hierarchy, by *Parsifal,* which you played again and again on your mother's record player. Alchemical operations performed to musical accompaniment, occult opinions about colour of the sort that Steiner or Kandinsky, following in the scented wake of Madame Blavatsky, made stylish among artists once upon a time, one not as remote or without afterglow as you might think — none of these affections of youth and early manhood preoccupied you any longer. You accepted the scientific method and democracy, and forgot about electrical vitalism, the doctrine of correspondences, mesmeric or sidereal influences, Wagner.

Here, Nylons said, rising from his perch on the edge of the matrimonial bed. He crossed to the counter on which he had dropped the sacks of food, and drew from them sausages and cheese. He sliced bread, put the slices and the other food on a dirty plate, there being no other kind in the studio, and put the plate of food on the drawing table. Here, he said, eat this. Drink this, he said, pouring beer into a glass. Jupp sat and ate and drank. This happened a week before today, when the weather is unusual.

⌒4

Alexander wishes to know more about the studio. I oblige him, though his demands for knowledge have lately become incessant. A sheet and a grey military blanket are strewn on the massive unmade bed. An unpainted wooden chair stands beside a battered, enamelled metal table, which Jupp bought from a trafficker in furnishings meant for clinics and sick rooms. A naked bulb depends from a plaster oak-leaf wreath of victory that had been applied, in another century, to the ceiling high overhead. Neither his body nor the crockery and cookware heaped into the sink has been washed in weeks. He forgets to flush the toilet. Like the sheet on the mattress, the walls of the studio and his underwear were once white.

He sits on the wooden chair, lights a filterless cigarette, takes a long, deep drag, slowly exhales the smoke into the close air of the studio. He looks at the blackened, tightly and well made box. That he cannot admire the box's honest craftsmanship, that he cannot admire anything, might trouble him, were he ready to remember anything that pleased him before 1945, which he is not.

So because he cannot do it now, you remember the pleasure he took, as a boy and youth in Kleve, in anything that possessed mechanical exactitude, such as well-joined boxes, such as the alarm clocks he screw-drivered into heaps of gleaming gears and pins on the kitchen floor. Remember his admiration, when just nineteen, for the Luftwaffe's radio equipment he learned to operate after signing up in the summer of 1940, roused from lethargy and his intense boredom with little Kleve and everything in it, even his drawing, by the German invasion of the low countries. Remember the Luger semi-automatic pistol he learned to aim accurately and fire during his military training. I have held a Luger in my hand, and remarked to a bystander on the weapon's sleek, precise and efficient design, its manly fit to the grip.

Too, remember the JU 87 dive bomber he flew in during the war, remember that he wanted to pilot it, to caress the controls as a pilot does, commanding the plane's trajectory and speed and altitude, but was never allowed to, perhaps due to defective eyesight—his biographer speculates thus. He could, and did, however, serve in the air as a radio operator. In his seat behind the pilot, he heard the JU 87's appalling wail when the pilot plunged the plane toward the earth, loosed the small cache of explosives on columns of enemy soldiers or on defensive emplacements, yanked up the aircraft out of the lethal parabola just short of the ground, brought it buzzing into the freedom of the upper sky.

Understand that, since 1945, he has forgotten the pleasure he formerly took in dismantling clocks, in the JU 87's howling swoop down upon enemies, and in the man's martial body that years of marching, camping, training, singing with the Hitler Youth turned his boy's slender body into. Understand, too, that in the decade that has passed since the war's end, he has known nothing of guilt. The thought that any German male of his generation should harbour remorse will not occur to him until the 1960s, when fame makes him a quarry of contentious quotes, much resorted to by lazy West German and American journalists and critics, and then he will reject the idea.

I remember nothing bad about the war, and I regret nothing, he will tell reporters at the thronged press conference, his face strobed by igniting flashbulbs. The war, he will say, was an adventure undertaken by millions of young Germans at the time, people who believed, as Americans and Britons believed and still believe, that a man should defend and serve his homeland in its season of crisis. The war, hard as it was, gave many men opportunities to show courage, selflessness, and loyalty. Whatever else can be said about it, the war was valuable life-experience, he will say. And the reporters will gratefully scribble down his comments in their notebooks, set them at the top of their stories about the press conference, go out for beer with other reporters after the story is filed, just before the deadline, convinced that the line is sufficiently outrageous to boost the story to page one.

I am sure I could have made it to the front page with this quote, unless my editor prejudiciously found the rest of the report unbalanced, as he probably would have, had I been a journalist in the 1960s, which I was not. Can't you find anyone to say this guy is full of garbage? the editor would have spluttered at me as the minute-hand of the office clock inched toward the vertical position, signalling the hour of dead-line, which was very near.

I could not have found anyone, because I would not have tried to do so. Had I been a reporter at the time, I would have let the grown-man Jupp go on and on, telling of the good things he experienced during the war — the travel to interesting destinations far from narrow, Catholic, petty-bourgeois Kleve, comradeship with decent, hardy fellows — and nothing about the bad things he did not experience, did not witness, that nobody, even the hostile biographer, can prove he witnessed, let alone perpetrated. I would have let him tell his story, which deserves a place on the shelf opposite the Manichaean narratives of the war put about by the victors since 1945, ones that say every German soldier in-flicted horrors, or colluded in them, or knew about them and did nothing to stop them, or knew about them and put them out of his mind. Jupp remembered everything he had seen and known, except, at Cuxhaven and since, certain things that pleased him before the war and during it, such as the exactness of a Luger, one of which I have held in my hand.

On the sidewalk outside his window, a teenaged girl may be listen-ing to her radio, singing along to the melodies. The woman in the leatheroid trench coat has probably changed the subject, is no longer telling the two veterans how bad the movies are, is talking about some-thing else that means nothing. The boy has resumed the spurling of his yo-yo toward the sidewalk, where it walks-the-dog. If these people are there, if they are doing things, Jupp hears the sounds coming from the sidewalk outside his studio, but does not try to make sense of them.

~ 5

Until recently, Jupp could at least feel disgust, which is close to exhilaration, and sometimes he was disgusted.

Just after the war, he winced at midnight when dodging a negro GI who cuddled Miss Veronika Dankeschön (as Germans called every countrywoman who fraternized with the occupiers, having picked up the contemptuous expression from the GIs themselves). The couple, she without shame, stumbled out of a jazz club's neon haze and weaved away past Jupp down a lane. Alexander says he does not think anything like this actually took place, but I assure him it did.

Jupp was startled one morning to notice, for the first time — why this had never before occurred to him, I cannot say — the utter absence from a reconstructed city square of Catholicism, the Gothic façade, the memorial statuary, the half-timbering he remembered from boyhood. All of it had been bombed, the smithereens and charred planking hauled off, then all of it replaced at some point after the war by architecture in the style of nowhere. He was revolted aesthetically, at a depth very close to that of politics. Having no politics, he could not frame the sensation, the nausea, in language, so he felt it as an attack on a wordless suburb of himself, painful, unremitting. But now, on a winter day early in 1956, he no longer feels anything like that species of disgust, which has become as foreign to him as ecstasy. He feels carnal pain in his leg, his head.

He twists in the chair now and again. His injuries bother him. I will not exaggerate the number or nature of these war wounds, which the biographer counts as two, one serious. When he tries to sleep, which can be any time of the day or night that exhaustion overtakes him, the grenade fragments buried in his leg wake him up, like dogs barking at cats in an alley. His head, cracked in a plane crash on the eastern front in 1944, has healed, knitted itself together long ago, but he sometimes senses that his brain is bleeding into the tump of his skull. When he goes to the beery reunions of his Luftwaffe unit, he always wears the military honours awarded him for injury in combat.

He sits on the wooden chair and smokes and looks at the box, while people on the sidewalk below his window talk. They talk about important things or unimportant things, mostly unimportant, since, like most other adult Germans in 1956, they believe in nothing. They talk perhaps because they have things to talk about, perhaps not. He hears their voices, but he does not listen to what they say. I disapprove of his smoking.

I disapprove of Sister's smoking, too, but my opposition has never stopped her. She smokes when she writes, and she smokes more than usual when finishing one of her books that I do not read. When her priest visits the house, she shares cigarettes with him, who does not smoke in the company of any woman other than Sister. They sit and smoke and talk on the south porch in the summer afternoons and, when cold weather comes, in the drawing room with tall French doors. Roses bloom in our grandmother's garden beyond the south porch, throughout the summer, but Sister and the priest do not talk about them, I think. I think they talk about other things, things that tie them to themselves and to each other, about which I choose to know nothing. I do not approve of their friendship, or their smoking. I trust that Alexander, who is a sensible child, will never adopt Christianity or take up smoking, both vices.

The pain of Jupp's injuries never leaves him. At certain times of the year, it worsens. Lately, the pain has not worsened. He has not worked in weeks. He formerly drew obsessively, making laconic sketches of a tall girl, a green girl, a girl knee-deep in water, a pregnant girl, a prancing girl, a girl with antlers. Since Christmas, he has not drawn the girl or anything else. For a while, he sat at the table in his studio for hours, blank sheets before him, charcoal stub in hand, waiting for the hand to drop and the stump of char to leave a mark. He does so no longer.

~6

Across the river this afternoon, at a counter in the post office, the woman weighs a wrapped book addressed to a street in Manchester, announces the postage due to an austere, well turned-out gentleman in advancing years, a dealer in rare volumes who, in the 1930s, discreetly circulated books by Heine among select clients and friends after his, Heine's, banning by Reich censors. He hands over the requested payment, the exact amount. She affixes the postage . Behind the counter are two canvas bags, open at the top, one for domestic mail, the other for foreign parcels. Absent-mindedly, thinking of something else, she almost drops the parcel bound for Manchester into the domestic bag, but notes her mistake in time not to make it. She is tired of weighing parcels, affixing postage stamps, dropping them into the right bag. Her mind wanders forward to the end of the working day, when she will meet two girlfriends, also employees at the central post office, walk to the UFA-Palast and watch newsreels, American cartoons, and, for the second time, *Prince Valiant,* starring Robert Wagner.

The woman who works in the post office, who did exist, but about whom the biographer discovered nothing, not even a name, wears a trim little uniform and flat shoes, no jewellery apart from a purely ornamental crucifix — she believes in nothing — little makeup, nothing in her auburn hair, which is done in a swirly cut, like a starlet's. Compared to the actresses in the Hollywood features she likes to watch, she is plain, but not unlovely, and some men have found her freckles adorable. She is infatuated with Robert Wagner. Later this evening, after the movie, after her return to the flat she shares with her mother, when she is alone, she will imagine Robert Wagner naked, a body in California burnished by sunshine and salt breezes, its contours and slopes firm and free of both sharp edges and fat.

She is not cruel. Undressing Robert Wagner in her mind, undressing herself, she will not think about Jupp's no longer desirable body. Looking at black and white soft-focus shots of the star in an American movie magazine, she will imagine herself clasped in Robert Wagner's muscular arms, held there against his chest willingly, tenderly, after his combat with evil is done, kissed deeply in this sensuous moment like the lady of the age of chivalry she is not.

Jupp met the woman during the Carnival season in early 1955, at a party produced by his friend, known as Nylons, whom I have invented by cobbling together fragments of information about someone real and about bohemians I have only heard of, having never met one. People gave him the nickname right after the war, when the cities were still in ruins, because he always had American-made stockings to hand on to girls he wanted to sleep with, and nobody could figure out where he got them.

He met Jupp during Jupp's first term at Düsseldorf's art academy, in 1946. When someone remarked that Nylons was doing something kind — he neither condescended nor patronized, and he was caught very seldom — he always said, off-handedly, that he collected men and women and youths as sources for his fiction and poetry. He could, he went on, distract himself from the emptiness with bird-watching or mushroom-hunting, but people were more interesting, less predictably lawful than birds or mushrooms. Most of his friends ignored this masquerade, some even indulged him in it. But as they knew, the devil's mask he wore wasn't totally false. He was a seducer. He lacked, that is, the confidence that someone could love what he was. He could not be *American* enough.

So, though he had little in the way of conventional good looks, he used all the equipment he possessed to capture the people he wanted in his entourage. He had feral sexual style, which intrigued some women. He baited his hook for men and women with musical knowledge and literacy: After the war, he was always the first in his little crowd to acquire the latest bop recording from the United States (Charlie Parker, Lester Young, Thelonious Monk), and he made a point of knowing the latest utterance by the avant-gardist Parisian writers who patronized Les Deux Magots. He could dance the American dances as soon as they were broadcast on the American Forces Network. He concealed the main points of his patrician education in Latin, English and French authors and, of course, German ones, so that he was not more conspicuous than necessary in the company of the louche and the luckless, whose exploitation of him he endured without demur. I may explain, for Alexander's sake, in what this exploitation consists; or I may not.

Moreover, Nylons' political pedigree made him appealing to a certain post-war German taste for distance from all things Nazi. It was well known among his acquaintances that he had frequented the Waterloo cinema, in Hamburg's Dammtor district, where young Axel Springer screened popular American films for culturally deviant youth before Germany declared war on the United States; and that he had been taken into custody during the Gestapo's 1941 round-up of Hamburg's jitterbugging young wildfolk. The police had cut his long, wavy black tresses and destroyed the un-German homburg he wore for flair. They could well have designated him asocial or work-shy, and dispatched him, along with some other swing kids, to the labour camps. He wasn't dealt this fate, because — this part of his story was not well known after the war — he was hardly a ringleader of the swing kids, harboured no political opinions deemed dangerous by the regime, was not impudent during his polite but persistent questioning by a middle-aged Gestapo officer, and because his industrialist father had connections with the state and hence with the police. Immediately after this episode, Nylons took himself off to the Wehrmacht, in which he served without distinction, but with luck.

Meanly, but sufficiently, ensconced in Düsseldorf by his wealthy mother after his discharge from a French prisoner-of-war camp, Nylons pursued a jobless life of pleasing himself in the bare post-war years. He smoked American cigarettes and drank American spirits — so the biographer avers — read the German authors whose work had been suppressed by the Nazis, and the new American writers whose work became available due to the Allies' project of forcefully baptizing Germany into the bourgeois-democratic church of modernist history. By 1950, he had read Joyce and Gottfried Benn and the Manns. He remained clean-shaven, never letting his beard flourish into a black, scraggly nest. He probably tried, but if so rejected, the standard costume of the non-conformists, the long-sleeved black sweaters and dark, baggy slacks that, like the ceremonial attire of devout Muslim women, would have made his flesh a mystery to all but lovers. He occasionally wrote plotless stories and fragmented poems of lyric length, which he did not try to publish, about joys of soldiering and eros and about the sorrows of the usually broke painters, superannuated prostitutes and urban peculiars whose company he kept, and whom, in his fashion, he carefully looked after.

Jupp was neither louche nor luckless when Nylons met him in 1946 in the ruins of Düsseldorf. But Nylons saw in Jupp a flicker of sensibility behind the young man's small-town, small-time stylelessness, and he made up his mind to breathe it into a blaze. He did not succeed in this ambition, but he enjoyed trying. Nylons also liked, more than anything else, Jupp's adoration and attention, his willingness to be Nylons' reader and audience, the trusty, if socially illiterate, lieutenant to his literate captain when the two of them roamed for women, beer and knowledge in Düsseldorf's post-war cultural scene, which was then discovering itself, and which Jupp was discovering.

Nylons had seen the young woman in the post office, found her attractive, tried half-heartedly to seduce her, failed in the attempt. Nevertheless, something about her interested him — what he took to be her alpine, freshly tubbed clarity, the relief she promised from the urban drab toward which he otherwise gravitated. He talked to her whenever he went to the post office, which was often, because he was on the look-out for parcels of books and financially important letters from his mother in Hamburg. He invited the woman, in early 1955, to his Carnival party, which he represented as a gathering of just a few friends, nothing formal, nothing she needed to dress up for. Before she arrived, Nylons told Jupp she was coming, that she was something different, someone unlike the usual lover Jupp found at Düsseldorf's openings and readings. He thought Jupp might be interested, since he knew Jupp was looking for something different.

Jupp, who could not make small talk and knew no pick-up lines, told her he was an artist, a sculptor actually, a graduate of the art academy, and that he had carved some cemetery monuments, but wanted commissions to do memorials of the war dead and crucifixions. She asked if he ever made art about anything alive. Yes, all the time, he replied—drawings of elk and stags and swans and girls.

Swans? she asked, trying to read his preference in love. She did not know much about Nylons or his social scene, but she could tell from the crowd at the party that he surrounded himself with male and female sexuals of several kinds, only one of which, male and heterosexual, amused her at any level deeper than anthropological curiosity.

Jupp's chest was deep, unostentatiously muscular. He did not stoop or fidget, his azure eyes gazed fixedly. He bore his maleness lightly, not like some other German men she had known, for whom being the males they had to be was a kind of injury. His hands were large, more than an octave wide, indelicate. His eyes were as unrevealing as they are in the photograph I have. In that moment of questioning, his style of longing remained opaque to her.

Girls? she asked.

Especially girls, Jupp said.

~ 7

The female who would grow up and work in the post office after the war huddled with her mother and sisters in an air-raid shelter, when the Allies shelled and bombed Düsseldorf for the last time.

Then a morbid quietness in the city, then voices at the mouth of the bunker, shouting orders in a language she did not understand, but knew was English. Her father came home from the front, and was quiet for a long while. She underwent puberty and filled out a couple of years after the war ended, thinking that all men were quiet, the German men and boys she knew at least, until the screenings of Hollywood movies resumed in the newly-reopened or rebuilt cinemas. Then she saw sun-lit men from California who, like the GIs she glanced at side-wise on the streets and in shops, seemed more eager than German boys to possess a girl who wanted, like the women in Hollywood romances, to be possessed.

When Jupp possessed her in the huge oak-framed bed in his studio —the woman did not know men other than those who peopled her fantasies—she interpreted his roughness, the anxious haste of his love-making, as expressions of the male ardour she had witnessed in the Hollywood movies she liked to watch. Then he was more than hasty, but I will not write about that, being intent, as I am, to write only about matters Alexander will understand. She did not fathom the anger. She appealed to him to tell her what angered him, and he told her he did not know what she was talking about. He said things would be different once they became engaged, so they became engaged.

She broke off the engagement at Christmas, 1955, a few weeks before this Saturday. It is factually true that a woman, name unknown, did this, then. It is not known if she told Jupp she did not want to see him again after the two of them had been to the movies, to watch *The Song of Bernadette*. I do not approve of this Hollywood film. It is based on the popular novelized account (1941), by the Jew and former Expressionist writer Franz Werfel, of Bernadette Soubirous' transfiguration at Lourdes from a small-town French girl, somewhat slow and certainly dismal, into a fabulously famous saint, the result of an intervention in French provincial history by the Blessed Virgin Mary, who allegedly came from God bearing instructions. What I say about the book and film is true.

Werfel should not have opined about Christian topics, of which he knew nothing, could know nothing, whatever *frisson* he experienced during his 1940 visit to Lourdes *en route* to America. Anyway, religious movies, religions themselves, especially Christianity, Christianity above all, are escapist sentimentalizations of the death-instinct. Thinking men find all of it disagreeable — sacred films and Bibles and popes, the lot — except when religion proves to be useful for the maintenance of public order, or an instrument for curbing maverick passions, which amounts to the same thing. Ideally, a man should accept death and defeat, the inevitable accompaniments of the ceaseless struggle that is the fate of every species, every race, everything alive, including nations, though the South could have fought on for its cause beyond downfall in 1865. There could have been, should have been, guerrilla warfare, for example, but segregation did ensue, which perpetuated certain aspects of slavery under another name for a hundred years.

I am not reactionary. I believe, and have written, that the dark race, in a future South freed from both Christian superstition and Enlightenment rationality, would be educated to appreciate its primordial traditions, the ones that predate the coming to Africa of Christian missionaries, European imperialists, Islamic slave-traders. It would be tutored in the narratives and liturgies and folkways that have been salvaged by anthropologists from the ruins of its savage dawn-time, when the race was innocent and manly and clean. There would be no music. The dark race has no business learning to read anything more complex than mottos and regulations, since the primitive mind is bored by Proust and Tolstoy and Cervantes.

8

But such thoughts uncompose, discomfit me. They did not do so
formerly. Now I must compose myself, I must be composed if I am to
continue this writing, this entertainment for Alexander. I must be as
composed as Sister is, who wears white cotton dresses when she sits on the
porch during hot, cloudless summer afternoons, entertaining with lem-
onade and talk the people who have read her stories and come long ways
to visit her. Sister is always composed. She is composed when she writes,
which she does every day, except Sunday, from noon until dinner time,
then again after dinner until far into the morning, long after I have
retired. I do not know when she sleeps, if she sleeps at all, and she is
famous because she is sleepless and always composed, as I am not.

When I asked her, many years ago, how to write, she said, Write
the truest thing you know. When, for a long while, no one would publish
what I had written, she told me to go on writing the truest thing I knew
until I believed it, or could believe it no longer. The truest thing I know
is that the glory of Jupp's mature sculptures, installations and countless
works on paper is contested only by obtuse observers. Even his most
militant critics, even the biographer who detests him, cannot ignore what
Clement Hsi has called his art's prominence in post-war European cultural history, the gravity and intelligence of the works to be found today
in collections at Darmstadt, Kleve, Schloss Moyland, Berlin. To admire
his sculpture — monumental, commemorative — is to court reproach only

in the international art world's rarified, radical-leftist circles, or from his most recent biographer, who uses the words heroism and beauty as accusations.

I have now composed myself. I have learned not to fear reproach. I have learned to compose myself by writing the truest thing I know. Jupp composed himself by making the truest things he knew, could sense, could touch with his hand and mind. He made a ponderous bronze tub, which Sister and I saw in the German town of Kleve, in a museum fashioned from the bath-house of an extinct spa. It's not a tub, Sister said. It's a commemorative statue of a tub formerly resorted to by arthritics, victims of polio, the palsied and hamstrung in search of remedy and solace — a very stern, solid, authoritative tub within which the fragile and injured bather could feel safe, as it is the clinic's task to make him feel. The tub is in a museum that was once a clinic dedicated to the treatment of such people, Sister told me, so it is at home here, she said, and I listened to her words about the tub. Art is the clinic of Being, I think she said, and I think I heard her say that.

At the time, pausing beside her in the sunken gallery where the tub-like sculpture was displayed, I was unimpressed. Sister had always talked like this, making much of little, ever since we were children in the house of our grandmother. But Sister's words, which I did not understand in the beginning, haunted me down through the months she and I lived in Europe, then during the years after we returned to the South, where I thought about the tub constantly.

Her words come back to me as I write these notes in my room at the Occidental Hotel, where she will never think to look for me. The words of my sister, whatever they mean, warm me a little — I have been cold since checking into this place — and the cold reminds me of the tub, and what she said about it. I think of other words, some of which are my own, some of them from the notebooks about Jupp I kept since seeing the tub in Kleve. Assuming the high style of a real writer, one of a sort different from Sister, whose writing is flat, unsalted, I can name the forthright masculinity of Jupp's art, its evocation of chthonic forces (thermal and fluid and even political), a spa tub's soothing of minds tormented by the noise of colliding systems. The tub comes from the

Romanticism that for centuries nourished the irrational, higher-seeking soul of German culture and starved the rationalist seedlings of the poisonous tree known as the Enlightenment.

I loved the tub then, it filled me with fully-fledged words, so I grieved as I read the huge biography of Jupp. I do not dispute the facts that the writer has excavated from archives, the nearly innumerable facts marshalled in this book — about Jupp's boyhood and youth in Kleve during the 1930s, about his war-time service with the Luftwaffe in Eurasia and in Europe, about his training with the sculptor Ewald Mataré in Düsseldorf after the war and his spectacular and controversial career in academia, the art world and German politics after 1960. What troubles me is not this or that bit of evidence in the narrative, but rather the miasma of innuendo that fogs this book, the incessant twisting of every fact into an indictment of the artist's character, the contention that if we knew the artist as he, the biographer, now knows him, we would hate him, and dismiss as charlatanry the greater part of his legacy.

Take, for example, I tell Alexander, the assertion that, because Jupp enacted in his career after 1956 the theatricality and philosophy he had grown up with in National Socialist Germany, the world, especially the art world, should have relentlessly shamed him for doing so, rather than turn him into an incessantly photographed celebrity. I write in defense of the courage and loyalty with which Jupp met the challenges of youth and early manhood. I am qualified to speak, because my body, like Jupp's, was shaped in the womb of embattled cultural ideas, in my case those of a family grounded centuries deep in the American South. There, in the place of my conception, I was infused with respect for the dignities and achievements of noble souls in the past, and by dislike for most of what travels on the passport of modernity. In my early life, in the library of my grandfather, I, like Jupp during the Third Reich, learned to revere discipline, stalwartness, physical endurance. I would inculcate, by good example, these virtues in Alexander, who, like me, has never been to school with children of the ordinary sort, or of any sort.

In creative matters, too, I found myself disposed from an early age to value useful art — mnemonic, literary and monumental art — over the decorative products of aesthetic whim and decadent intellectual fancy. I cherished clean fatherhood and manliness in all their dimensions, and I admire art that is cleanly fathered by manly men. In my writing, I bless the forces that nurtured my consciousness in the inner South, which is a moral style, not a place on the map, the flourishing of which was cut brutally short by the armies of the United States. I came into the world almost too late to know, first hand, this defeated but defiant state of mind—something that is not a tattered, best-forgotten memory, but, like the German culture that nurtured Jupp, a forcefully cancelled, but still allusive, experiment in alternative civilization.

I make no apology for these opinions, though they have made brief the list of my published works outside the odious Southern nationalist journals that have seen fit to issue my work from time to time. I cannot change the desperate Southern sun into the moon, and I cannot change the topic of my writing, which is the baleful career of modernity, into something more saleable. I do not need to be reminded, since I am aware of the proposition's bitter truth, that were I to write something of a lewd nature, the smuttier and more delicious the better, I could see millions of copies stamped with my name rolling off the presses, without a single censorious finger raised to stop them—the hunger for such material being bottomless in America, the deadly tolerance for it pervasive. But offend the ill-mannered humanism, the mediocrity and indifference, the *bien pensant* intellectual immorality of this age, and see how quickly the editor issues a rejection slip.

∽9

Jupp smokes in the studio on a Saturday early in 1956. Since Christmas, he has wanted little other than cigarettes and the box he ordered and paid for. Not more than a little food, not a woman or a man, not wine, not the lustre of a winter day as unusual as the people on the sidewalk are saying this one has been. I disapprove of his smoking.

The box stands in the middle of the studio, and Jupp looks at it while he sits and smokes. The sun drops below the horizon, which is not visible out the window, sinks from the numinously pale blue, blankly staring afternoon sky into darkness. The brief, early winter dusk slides like fog over Heerdt's sometimes flooded river embankments, into streets and laneways, and into the studio, so he switches on the light that hangs over the table. After sitting and smoking under the bright, nude bulb for another hour, by the end of which the street has become dark, he stubs out the cigarette in a saucer of butts and ashes, stands up.

He shucks his stout work boots and woollen socks, his white shirt and brown trousers, his underpants jaundiced by urine, underwear he has not changed in weeks, then sits down again, completely naked, as men become in this age when they intend to make love. I have not been naked. My father begot me while naked, I am sure of it, because, when I was a very little boy, in a motel on the frayed edge of a city in the South, I saw him, naked, struggle or play a rough sport with a white woman I did not know.

Not that I understood what he did at the time, or had a name for it. But I wanted him to do it to me, whatever it was, because doing so seemed to agitate and please him, and I wanted to please him. Why does he do this to a woman unknown to me, my little boy's mind wondered as I watched him and sipped the orange juice I had been given, but not to me? Some time later, I deduced from the low talk of male cousins who sometimes visited me, and from the book for boys my grandmother commanded me to read when down appeared on my upper lip, that he had also done it to my mother in the darkness, begetting me. From the hour I obtained this knowledge, my principles have been inviolate, whatever shameful acts have been performed upon me by others. Though I live among mongrels and effeminates, I have kept my distance, remained loyal to my race, which is white and dry and clear, which is my destiny.

The clothing Jupp has taken off is stylishly proletarian, well-fitted across the chest and tight in the seat and about the male organs of replication, pants cut according to the American manner affected by young German men in the mid-1950s, though, at 36, he is no longer young. His clothes are not those of a poor man. When he still could, before he stopped drawing and sculpting, he earned a meagre living from commissions for grave markers, occasionally sold graphic work and souvenir-sized sculptures carved or moulded after precedents in esoteric Christian art. His mother sends him money. Nylons pays for the groceries he fetches in from the shops.

Without making a noise, Jupp slips from the chair to the bare floor. He crawls alongside the box. He bends his knees and elbows and bows his back until he is curled small, scoots his naked body into the box, and pulls the door shut, latches it.

With the door closed and fastened, he cannot hear the voices he has heard but not listened to. The air inside the box is dark and hot. He smells tar and his own stink.

~ 10

Götz, scrawny as Envy in old books of allegorical emblems and unmentioned in the biography, meanders alone and without a destination by the damp-stained plastered house the studio is in, because he does not know what he would like to do or with whom he would like to do it. He is a wanton, and neither Alexander nor I like him. He glances, out of habit, at the properties he supervises for the owner, checking on their appearance, for no particular reason, in the dusk now becoming night. He notices that the light in Jupp's studio is on. During this evening's stroll, he has not thought of Jupp before this moment. The lilt and warmth of this unusually mild mid-winter evening make him lazy about business. But he is slowed, reluctantly, by the moral idea that he should knock on the lacquered green door of Jupp's house, pounce on him about the month's rent, which is overdue, and perhaps get out of him certain information he requires. Götz wants to walk by, but he is reasoning now, and this process of consciousness, to which he is not accustomed, stops him.

Were he to knock, Götz reasons, Jupp would perhaps not open the door to him, because he opens it seldom these days. Götz learned this detail from one of Jupp's female acquaintances, another artist, who dropped by Götz's office and said she believed Jupp was dead because nobody had answered the door in two weeks. She knew he was upset about something, she did not say what, but it was not like him, she said, to disappear, go to ground, like that. Perhaps he is staying in the country, Götz said, perhaps he is preoccupied, it's none of my business. He thought for an instant she might be Jupp's lover, immediately decided she wasn't, unless he had recently acquired her, since she, the artist, was not the woman he saw Jupp with frequently before Christmas, coming and going. She replied politely: Would Herr Götz kindly check on Jupp at least once and let her know he is all right?

To have an excuse to contact the female artist, who interested him, Götz rapped on the green door one morning, got no answer. He came back the next day, in the late afternoon, knocked, and this time Jupp answered the door, opening it a cautious crack, then, when he saw his disturber was Götz, pushing it open wider. Perhaps because he was apprehensive — though his rent was paid, and he had no cat, possession of which was outlawed — Jupp asked Götz his business abruptly, and Götz explained the circumstances of his mission, how Jupp's silence had worried a young woman, and you can't worry a young woman without something happening. He then said his job was done, Jupp being alive, and said that he would be on his way. But before he turned from the door, Jupp asked him where he had served.

Götz was about to reply that this was not Jupp's concern, that he did not think about the war in any case, when Jupp, without waiting for a reply, said he had been on the eastern front, and, near the end of hostilities, in a brutal, desolating artillery fight in the northern German forests, where he and the other tattered tag-ends of his decimated paratroop unit surrendered to the British in April, 1945. This fight is imaginatively described in the biography, so it actually happened. Götz said he had been captured in Tunisia in 1943, then shipped to a prisoner of war camp in Texas, where he was obliged to pick cotton under punishingly hot, boring blue skies and undergo political re-education until Germany's surrender, and for months thereafter.

The Americans weren't all bad in Texas, Götz said, loosening up. It was the Germans, the fanatics, who were up our ass all the time about it. There was this officer, captured the same time as me, I think he was from somewhere in Bavaria, I don't remember, and he told us, for a long time while the war went on, that we should never give up on it, that it was the truest thing there was, and the only hope in hell we had against the onslaught of Bolshevik apes from the east and negroes from America. Most of us just wanted to be left alone. But he talked and talked about it, said the idea of it was so strong we couldn't lose. Then we lost and he kept talking about it, as if nothing had happened. I don't know what became of him, after we were sent home in '47. Maybe he wrote a book.

In fact, he did write a book, about the Communist threat to Germany in the twenties and thirties, as Götz suspected he might, but not until many years after the war, toward the end of his life, toward the end of the Cold War, by which time the portrayal of Communism as great, intractable and unreformable evil had become stylish in Western political and ruling-class circles again. I read the big book by the former Afrika Korps officer years after it was published, when I was reading many war memoirs written by Germans late in life, before they had begun to dodder. The Soviet imperium had come unglued some years before I read the book, then shivered into so many little barbarian capitalist statelets, and nobody believed in Communism any longer, outside Cuba. When I read the book, which made Communism seem so important, I was reminded of a time in my adolescence, before Communism fell apart, when it was still demanding, lyrical, vast, beautiful with wind-riffled forests of crimson flags on May Day, brusque toward dyspeptic poets and painters — all foreigners to the Russian racial type, I concluded after reading Dostoevsky's *Devils*. Then, Communism still offered strong happiness of the comradely sort I dreamed about having on certain days in my youth, but not on others.

Standing in the half-closed doorway of the house Götz rents him, Jupp said that he, too, inside the compound at Cuxhaven, was given the usual sunny lessons about democracy, civil liberties and voting. The young, dauntless British lecturers, Oxford and Cambridge men who spoke perfect school-German, wanted to rid the prisoners of myths of identity we had absorbed on the playgrounds, at home by the wireless, in the company of Hitler Youth, of soldiers at the front. They wanted to implant into the prisoners new memories, by which we would thereafter recall our lives, and Germany's life to this point, as poisoned and ignoble. The instructors, or hardship, or weariness bleached from my mind the old memories of myself and Germany, of anything pleasing in me and in Germany before the war, during it, but they failed to install properly the new memories of the German past as a blighted, malign city ruled by madmen and fantasists, memories they had concocted in London for use on instructional occasions, he told Götz. Jupp left Cuxhaven in August, 1945, without the old memories of pleasure, or the new ones of the desolate city Germany had presumably become, and therefore had in himself, in his language, his longing, neither nostalgia nor remorse.

But now, in 1956, his body, inert since 1945, stirred, quickened, desiring the recollection of certain scenes, encounters, fabrics, linguistic textures, dialogues his mind forgot in Cuxhaven, but that had remained imbedded in the weft and weave of his frame. He cannot effect this resurrection of the body, not just now, as he sits inside the box. So I remember, as a brother or tender comrade might, and you, an accomplice in this project since you read the first line of it, remember the facts I have obtained from the biography and other sources, and from my precise, disillusioned thought about these facts, which thought has been tinted, tinctured by photographs, some of which may exist, by images of artworks, by Jupp's statements and what he left unsaid, undone.

Jupp told Götz he wanted to remember certain things, but he might be dying of starvation, though Nylons brought food to him most days. Götz thought, after Jupp had finished speaking: So this is what artists talk about, rubbish. He called the female artist who had piqued his appetite, told her Jupp was alive, just disinclined to have visitors these days. Any time she wanted company, however, she was welcome to stop by his, Götz's, office. She did not say she would not, though she was not heard from again.

⌒11

Götz stands, still reasoning, on the unseasonably warm street in front of Jupp's studio. Were he to knock, and were Jupp to answer the door, he, Götz, would ask for the money. One of three things will then happen

Jupp produces the rent money, in which case the business will be concluded, the door will shut, and Götz will have no occasion to engage Jupp in a conversation about the tastes and habits of the young Düsseldorf artist who asked him to check on Jupp, the girl who has not called on him, about whom he wants to know everything, having picked up what little he knows about artists from sensational magazines published by the Axel Springer concern. Two grown men can talk frankly about these things without prurience, Götz has decided.

Or Jupp says he does not have the money on hand, but will get it soon, in which case Herr Götz will be magnanimous and agree to wait, in return for Jupp's expert advice on the matter concerning him, Götz, that is. Götz will start the questioning with a frank admission of his desire for the girl and of his need for Jupp's help, things one man can say without embarrassment to another, if he senses that the other man is game for intimate conversation about hungers.

Or Jupp says he does not have the money and has no way to get it, in which case Götz must become gruff and formal, refrain from asking about the female artist, and tell Jupp, in the name of the owner, a comfortably neurotic manufacturer of shoe polish, that he is to vacate immediately.

In the first scenario, Götz gets the money for the owner, but no reply to his pressing inquiries. In the third scenario, he gets neither money nor answers, and is faced with the prospect of trying to rent the dilapidated house, which he has had difficulty doing in the past.

Only in the second scenario does he earn the opportunity, by being generous, to pry into Jupp's store of privileged knowledge, get both the money (eventually) and the information (at once). He also avoids the task of trying to rent a mildewed, verminous house wanted by nobody, in his experience as the rental agent, other than the irresponsible — artists, eccentrics, problem children.

It should be torn down, he believes, and replaced by a smart new block of flats, any two of which would earn the owner more money than the house does. But the owner will hear nothing about demolition. The house had at one time been the home and studio of Andreas Achenbach, whom art historians call the father of nineteenth century German landscape painting, and whose silhouette, name and widely separated dates (1815–1910) are engraved on a stone placket affixed to the plastered wall beside the green door. As the owner, who is anxious about his reputation after death and who studies Prussia's Wars of Liberation (1813–1815) as a hobby, likes to say: What monuments of German culture the Lancasters did not destroy, I won't, either. So Götz knows the house, however foul, will persist, its plumbing and wiring becoming ever more problematic, and that he will always have to see that it is rented.

Later in 1956, Götz will see his wish come true: the house will burn. This fact is in the biography. The author asks rhetorically if Jupp torched it, with the clear implication that he did or could have done so. He produces no evidence of arson, so the impression is left, here as throughout the book, that Jupp was maliciously unhinged, perhaps even psychotic, during the season of his mental distress, and perhaps long afterward. This sort of thing is what I resent about the book: The omnipresent suggestion of wrong-doing, the presumption that, because Jupp had joined the Hitler Youth and fought with the Luftwaffe, because, after his breakdown in 1956, he was without guilt about those happily-remembered memberships, he was therefore capable of committing any crime, including arson, when, in fact, he was no more guilty of anything than millions of Germans his age who were loyal and brave and unashamed.

⌒ 12

The unwelcome thought of trying to rent the house prompts Götz to recall the immediate problem, that of obtaining the rent from the current tenant, who may have information vital to his, Götz's, gratification. But the evening air is soft, even if the ground still smells of winter, too quiet to interrupt with business, and, anyway, his lust for the artist is merely smouldering, not burning as brightly as he would wish. If he does not obtain information about the artist tonight, the missed opportunity might be unimportant, after all. In fact, perhaps she is not as interesting as he thought at first. And she is an artist, and he has heard about artists, read about them in the magazines, so she might be too esoteric or too weird for his taste, which runs, in matters of bed, to startlingly sudden entrances and exits. Perhaps, after all, he does not really need information about the girl tonight, she is probably busy anyway, so why bother — though Jupp should surely be dunned for the rent. The light is on, suggesting Jupp is home, but Götz is undecided. He hesitates, and so is lost.

I now show Alexander a square-shouldered, solid but small-breasted woman with short red hair, who does not exist outside this writing, who emerges from the apartment house next door to Jupp's studio. She has seen the skinny figure of Götz from her window. Now she advances on it, catches the sleeve of Götz's green jacket, then asks testily, for the second time in a week, when he intends to fix her toilet, which gasps hoarsely upon being flushed, and does not fill properly.

Before and during the war, Ulrike Slomka led classes in rhythmic gymnastics for young women in the League of German Maidens' Faith and Beauty organization. She stretched the women, bent them into cursive shapes, directed their undulations and curls and extensions, advised them on the coordination of mind, musculature and music, and occasionally slept with them. Now, in 1956, she teaches strenuous weight-reducing exercises to middle-class women who have been recently enriched a little too much by West Germany's economic miracle, and whose husbands are finding hefty.

Alexander should know that Ulrike had wanted, since the onset of adolescence in Berlin in 1926, and her attendance, the same day, at a performance by the avant-gardist Mary Wigman, to become a dancer. Her mother dispatched her to ballet classes, where she learned about *tours chaînés déboulés* and the *pas assemblé* until the Depression closed the school. She considered this no great loss, since, following Wigman, she would be modern, barefooted, sinuously muscled, long-limbed under frail chiffon drapery cut in a manner imagined to be ancient and Greek. In the summer of 1933, street fighting between browns and reds continued to erupt sporadically, despite the Nazis' recent attainment of power. Too, her father, a fashionable gynaecologist and a newly-minted Nazi, wished to consider himself and his family advanced. For these reasons, and because she begged to go, Slomka's father shipped her and her things off for the summer to the Austrian dancing school reigned over by Elizabeth Duncan, the sister and representative on earth of Isadora.

The academy was headquartered in the spiritlessly baroque, secluded Schloss Klessheim, which had been raised by bishops in a great park near Salzburg during the eighteenth century. The aim of the Duncan-Schule, Elizabeth explained to the girls on their first morning in the studio, was the transformation of awkward youngsters into beautiful vessels brimming with energies hitherto stifled by bourgeois propriety, now obsolete. Dance in the twentieth century, she went on, must be emancipated from the decadent, frigid rationalism of classical ballet. The female body must be freed from the tyranny of male dancing-masters, allowed to pulse according to its own imperatives, which are not those of men. In our art, she declared, this is the hour of the blood, the feminine, organic and chthonic faculties — of woman's soul, not the executive mind. You students, she reminded them, will be training hard, not merely to be graceful, physically fit adornments of future husbands — but also to become prophetic witnesses (as she called them) of the female body's self-discovery, its liberation from bourgeois shame.

Slomka, 17, was pleasantly surprised by Duncan's remark about the obsolescence of propriety, since she had been twisting uncomfortably within the confines of her home life, which was vigorously respectable. Her father brought home only properly brought-up, smartly dressed comrades for coffee and cake and conversation between 3 and 5 in the afternoon, never men of the street-brawling sort, and the teatime visitors always bored her. She heard about fights and parades on the nearby Kurfürstendamm, but only via rumours that leaked into her shady side-street in Wilmersdorf and the newspaper stories her parents talked about at breakfast. For this protected child, Nazism in 1933 meant certain clothing: the brown uniforms of the strangers her father and mother entertained at dinner more frequently, the starched collars and cuffs of straight-spined young men, medical students and freshly-fledged doctors, who talked with her father about getting on and prospering in the new order of things, and the pale linen suits — smartly, revealingly tailored, Ulrike noted, about the bust and hips — that Magda Goebbels wore when, in the summer of 1933, she began to come to the house for long, closed-door visits with Dr. Slomka, formerly just her gynaecologist, now her confidential advisor on sexology (for her husband, the Reich minister, was a philanderer). Ulrike knew little and did not care to know more about the national revolution, though she liked to watch, from a high window, on the mornings the minister's wife came to call, Frau Goebbels' high-heeled feet and long, silk-stockinged legs swing out of her chauffeured limousine, which motion occasionally exposed more female skin to the girl's secret view than the lady would have liked.

Sitting cross-legged on the floor of the studio, attending more closely to the erotic subcurrent than to the text of Elizabeth Duncan's speech, Ulrike decided that she was going to like her summer at Schloss

Klessheim. For the first time since her tiresome ballet classes ended — her household in Wilmersdorf was full of boisterous brothers — she would be in all-female company at every moment, only now those moments were to go on for many weeks. And at last, she thought, she was about to become the dancer she had always, post-Wigman, wanted to be.

She practiced complex moves with other girls in the studio in the palace's great entrance hall, which was encrusted with elaborate baroque plasterwork by Paolo d'Allio and Diego Francesco Carolone. Between drills, or breathing exercises, or difficult improvisations overseen strictly by Duncan, she would retreat with the other girls for a brief rest and an apple under the hall's soaring Roman archways. She would later dine on spartan fare with her classmates in a room with tall, pale walls that gently curved instead of sharply cornering, and, after dinner, stroll in the English garden at twilight with her favourites. Whether moving to music without shoes, and nude except for scarves and the merest scraps of costumery needed for decency, or taking breaks with the other students, or having an intimate tête-à-tête about nothing in particular with the raven-haired, long-bodied creature from Vienna whom she especially liked, or, exhausted by the day's exertions, slipping gradually through the day's final fantasies of love into sleep on the narrow, hard bed in the dormitory, Slomka adored her summer in 1933 with other teenaged girls at Schloss Klessheim, at least for a while.

Her excitement about it began to fade, however, when she started to realize that, while she tried to swing, drop, pitch and drive her body as nimbly and as energetically as any other girl at the school, she was not dancing as Duncan wanted. She forgot choreography, drifted off during Duncan's instructions in racial hygiene. Her mind occasionally went blank when Elizabeth Duncan ordered her to express with her body a certain moral mood, a sentiment, or to interpret, for instance, the apprehensive longing in a homoerotic love poem by Stefan George, a photograph of whom, dressed like Goethe, Duncan kept in her office. Slomka had, at least during the first weeks of the session, enjoyed the cult-like discipline of the school, the close-knit, subtly eroticized sorority of it, but by the end she had come to dread performance classes, which showed everyone, in her view, how unmusical she was.

Elizabeth took Ulrike aside, the week before everyone was to return home, into a high-windowed room with plastered walls the colour of ox blood, and told her that she would probably be happier in another vigorous activity, something more explicitly athletic, less artistically demanding, than dance. She complimented Slomka on her body, which was strong, if a little beefy, and perhaps short. Her red hair was nice. Don't be sad, my dear, Duncan said when Slomka began to cry. After all, the new dance is not for everyone. But you can still see it in Germany and love it as much as you want to, especially in Berlin. In fact, now that the Nazis are in, you'll soon be seeing more expressive dance everywhere in the Reich, since they understand what we've been trying to do for years. Here in Austria, she sighed, despite recent upheavals in Vienna moving the country in the right direction, old heads prevail. But Germany is another matter. Try gymnastics.

⌒13

Because she is extraordinarily fit for her age, and he is keenly attuned to fitness in women, Götz is inclined to be generous when beset by Slomka's complaints, which are actually signals that she wants love — a need she cannot communicate to Götz directly. She does not have this problem with the blooming, frank girls, who say they are fresh from the countryside, whom she meets at a certain fountain in Düsseldorf's Hofgarten, over whose bodies she lingers, unrushing, grazing. But at times she wants a man, just for a minute — or, to be specific, she wants one man, Götz.

Slomka discovered this fact one bleak winter afternoon in 1954, two years before Jupp retreats into his box, when Götz arrived at the door of her apartment after she complained, without ulterior motive, about a noxious smell in the hallway. He propositioned her. Surprised by his forwardness, and basically uninterested in men, she declined. He persisted, warmly saying things to her, about her, that were banal and vulgar, but that had the effect of making her untypically curious about the gangly body-parts she imagined lay underneath his loose sweater, behind his buttoned fly. He kissed her, she yielded to him, who unbuttoned himself, but did not become naked. Afterward, he said it had been nice, and left.

She does not plead with him. She thinks about him only when she wants him. After they make love, Slomka and Götz usually do not talk, since they have nothing to talk about and nothing heterosexually in common, other than a mutual liking for speedy love followed by a cigarette (for Götz; Slomka does not smoke), sometimes liquor (for both of them).

Götz's failure to respond to Slomka's first call for help, earlier in the week, was an uncommon lapse. Why should I, he thinks. Why not, he thinks. Götz draws a short sigh, does not knock on the green door of Jupp's house, then idles off with Slomka on the pretext of checking her ailing toilet.

Had Slomka not appeared, had Götz knocked, and, receiving no answer, concluded that his morbid tenant had indeed died of starvation and left the light on — Alexander must be clear about this — he would have let himself into the studio. Götz would then have seen the box and, from the rising and falling of breath and other barely detectable commotions, understood that Jupp or someone else was inside it. He would stare at it, transfixed by the desire to know how long Jupp or whoever could stay inside without suffocating. Jupp, if it be he inside, may suffocate, but this would be a matter of indifference to Götz, who does not like him. He talks too much.

Anyway, it is 1956, when many Germans, including wounded veterans, are enjoying success in business, finance, the arts, the professions. Stories about them surface in magazines all the time. Götz has no patience with Germans in their thirties who are not successes. Jupp, in Götz's view, is a German failure, a hypochondriac given to vaporous talk of memories and bodies, who is late on his rent. Götz has not absorbed the fact that he, Götz, is nothing more significant than the maintenance man and rental agent for an eccentric landlord, and, occasionally, a performer of consensual acts of love with one of the tenants. He considers himself to be significant. Nobody who is thinking about anything now, on the evening of this unusually mild winter day in 1956, except Nylons, thinks Jupp is significant. Few people outside Kleve, very few who live beyond the short shadow cast by Düsseldorf's art academy, have heard of him. Fifteen minutes from now, Götz will be panting atop Ulrike Slomka's firm body.

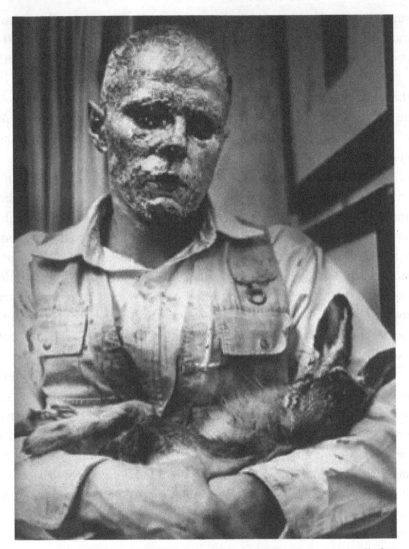

Figure 2: A photograph of Joseph Beuys taken during the Action called *How to Explain Pictures to a Dead Hare*, 26 November 1965, Galerie Schmela, Düsseldorf. The artist carried the hare's corpse around the gallery's basement in his arms. Beuys' head had been slathered with honey, then wrapped in gold leaf. The artist did not wear a hat on this occasion.

He looked like a man undergoing treatment for severe burns.

In Joseph Beuys, *trans. David Britt (New York: Abbeville Press, 1987) , page 135, Heiner Stachelhaus quotes the artist as follows: "For me the Hare is a symbol of incarnation, which the hare really enacts — something a human can only do in imagination. It burrows, building itself a home in the earth. Thus it incarnates itself in the earth: that alone is important. So it seems to me. Honey on my head of course has to do with thought. While humans do not have the ability to produce honey, they do have the ability to think, to produce ideas. Therefore the stale and morbid nature of thought is once again made living Honey is an undoubtedly living substance — human thoughts can also become alive. On the other hand, intellectualizing can be deadly to thought: one can talk one's mind to death in politics or in academia."*

On the morning of 3 February 1923, at Dornach, Rudolf Steiner was asked to comment on the effects of absinthe, and also on the difference between bees and wasps. The occult philosopher, in whose thought Joseph Beuys would become interested in 1937, ignored the first request, but addressed the second in remarks that, by year's end, had become the Nine Lectures on Bees *(trans. Marna Pease and Carl Alexander Mier, Spring Valley, New York: St. George Publications, 1975) The following lines appear in the first lecture:*

"I have already told you various things about the reproductive process and the unconscious wisdom contained in it. This unconscious wisdom is unfolded by the bees in their external activity. What we only experience when love arises in our hearts is to be found, as it were, in the whole bee-hive as substance … The individual bees renounce love in manifold ways, and thus develop love throughout the whole hive. One only begins to understand the life of bees when one knows that the bee lives in an atmosphere completely pervaded by love … [I]t feeds upon just those parts of the plants that are also wholly pervaded by love. The bees suck out their food — which they then turn into honey — exclusively from those parts of the plants that are centered in love; they bring, so to speak, the love-life of the flowers into the hive."

"When honey is eaten [Steiner continues] it furthers the right connection in man between the airy and the watery elements. Nothing is

better for man than to add the right proportion of honey to his food. For in a wonderful way the bees see to it that man learns to work with his soul upon the organs of his body."

Virgil, in the fourth book of his agricultural poem Georgics, *admires the beehive's marvellous society, one that is, he writes, puny in size, but glorious nonetheless. This sentiment joins the poet to a long procession of commentators, some older than he, many newer, who have found corroboration in the hive for their notions of perfectly regulated, efficiently productive political enterprise, whether monarchist, constitutional or republican, communitarian or corporatist. (Thomas Hobbes, dissenting from an opinion common among social philosophers of his own and later ages, believed that honeybee hives were not political in any sense, and so could teach us nothing about the right ordering of the state.)*

The bees gather incomparable sweetness from heaven, according to an ancient theory, and make the life-giving elixir of the immortal gods directly available to humankind. Eaten, honey extends life. Applied to a wound, it heals wonderfully. It also preserves meat from putrefaction. A tradition known to the first century, B.C., Roman geographer Strabo said the body of the dead Alexander the Great was put into a sarcophagus filled with honey. This story is likely false.

Honey is the stuff of eternal life. For Joseph Beuys, following Steiner, it represented the essence of the soul, or creative thought: the finest product of the mind's hive, the antidote to the poison of instrumental reasoning.

14

The truest thing I know is that, late in the summer my father was murdered, the Holy Spirit was believed by the credulous to have fallen at Spring Ridge, on the black people's church, a little one fashioned from pine planks and painted white, situated on an iron-red dirt road cut through the brush that edged my father's cotton fields. So one burning, close August afternoon in the South, I walked hand in hand with Essie, the black woman who looked after me, to Mr. Sam Hall's pond, not far from my father's house. Mr. Sam let Essie's people use the pond for baptisms after revival time each summer. We joined the black congregation by the water below the low green rise.

Because it was summer, the school bus no longer stopped on the road in front of the house to take me away. Because my mother had gone to live with her people in the city after her husband died, there was nobody to drive me anywhere, and no car to ride in, even had Essie been able to drive, which she was not. Sister, several years older than I was, had already gone away to school. I decided that the only way to find my father was to walk out. So I put Mr. Penguin into my lunch box each morning, took off the wall-peg the blind-man's cane my father had brought back from a hunting trip in Mexico, and headed for the front gate, where the black woman who minded me always waited, to stop me and lead me back up to the house. Her name was Essie.

No visitors stopped by Spring Ridge after our father died and our mother went to live in the city with her people, other than strangers who came by to see Mr. Willis, our father's overseer, on business. No children came to play with me, so I was alone with Essie throughout the bright days. Most afternoons, we carried bait, tackle and poles along the creek down to the Blue Hole and fished. Most days, I woke up at first light, before the rest of the house, and set out to join my father in the place he'd gone. Essie always stopped me.

～ 15

I sit at the window of my fifth-storey room at dusk. When not writing, I watch the faraway edge of the Occidental Hotel's parking lot, where the empty, flat asphalt expanse abruptly ends and the wilderness begins. White-tailed deer, incautious since summoned to rut by the shortening days, graze in the twilight on clover pushing up through cracks in the pavement. I wait to see if I can get off a good shot at a deer, which, if my aim is deadly, will give Mr. Steinway, Alexander and me meat for the winter.

On orders from the owner, whose existence is doubtful, Mr. Steinway switched off the power supply to the rooms (but not to the public areas of the building) after the people who had driven or hiked or hitchhiked in for the gathering of travelling folk checked out.

The aquamarine plastic wall-covering in my room is chilly to the touch. I sleep under several blankets.

⌒ 16

Down a narrow red-dirt cut in the green bush, the barefoot sinners marched single-file to Mr. Sam Hall's pond, each one of them robed in white from throat to ankle. They massed at the water's edge, a white cloud descending into the hot shimmer close to the green earth. From that white radiance black faces turned toward the sky, singing or praising, before going down into the water.

Eyes shut, arms crossed over bosom, body tenderly cradled by the preacher, each penitent sank slowly backward into the pond, disappearing into the warm gloom, then rose again into the sunshine. The white robes that had fallen in loose shrouds over the lost now moulded themselves wetly to the black chests and round bottoms of the saved. Where the blinding white cloud had rested only a moment before were singing men and women in wet robes, but whose names I knew, because they worked in my father's house or in the mule barn, or they chopped cotton in his fields.

In the great world, in the summer our father was murdered, the Cold War had begun, but, at Spring Ridge, the South my father came from had endured until he died. The gears of his truck whined when he picked up the field hands at their homes on red dirt roads every morning, and I came along. I could always tell, by listening to people, what voice of deference or mastery I should assume, and this was how it was when I was six. Black faces turned toward the dirt when my father spoke. On hot afternoons, my mother splashed Cara Nome toilet water on her throat. Burning slants of sunlight angled into the dusty interior of the cotton gin through intervals in the corrugated steel walls. I knew the law, and it was old, and it was the law I knew.

～17

Like Alexander's, in another part of the hotel, my room has aqua plastic wall-covering, pottery table lamps shaped like tall upended bobbins, thick white drapes. The travellers have departed, and the people temporarily employed as waiters and bellhops and cleaners have returned to their homes in nearby towns. There is no-one at the front desk to take my money, were I to offer it, which I do not, and there is no-one to tell me to pay up or leave. Mr. Steinway cannot be bothered with matters at the front desk. He has sequestered himself in his sunny office during daylight hours, preparing for an interview with a young historian of recently deceased resort hotels, poring over old-fashioned ledgers, letters and the diaries of former managers, texts, he says, that date back to the hotel's founding, deep in the twentieth century.

The freezers and pantries in the kitchen are still full of food— Mr. Steinway overstocked them for the congress of travelling folk, who did not eat as much as expected—so there is plenty for us to eat, for a while. I cook our meals in enormous pans and skillets, and bake bread in the enormous oven, and I will do so until the food runs out. It will run out soon. I wait with Mr. Steinway's rifle by the window of my room for a deer to wander by. The flesh of one buck will see us through the impending winter, or that is what I believe.

In the great world, everywhere beyond the perimeter of the Occidental Hotel, the Cold War is over. I have heard it said that the law of the Cold War has been repealed, replaced by famous laws with several names, accompanied by several legends, each one proclaimed by a state actor — president, demagogue, archpriest of the improbable — who is not to be believed. There is also a law of the edge, where creatures that are not wild and are not tame live, mate, hunt, feed. I watch the edge of the vast parking lot from the window of my room, watching and waiting for a deer to come by, grazing. I have heard and understood these legends and the theories about the era that has succeeded the Cold War, but I am of a mind to disbelieve them all. For right from the beginning, there was the law of the Occidental Hotel, as reasonable as arithmetic, and, running alongside it, there was always the law of the region closer to the edge, where creatures that are not wild and that are not tame, such as coyotes and bees, make homes for themselves. These laws persisted, twisting around each other, turning and twisting, after the end of the Cold War, after the stories ceased that had explained it. The legends and stories eddied now on the blue surface of time like the snapped twigs and catkins and trash that drifted and circled, pushed by deep currents of rising and falling water, on the surface of the Blue Hole, which was bottomless.

∼18

One morning late in the summer my father was murdered, I rose early and reached the gate and passed beyond it before Essie could catch me. I went along the creek to the Blue Hole. Everybody said it was bottomless. Drop something in, Essie once told me, and it was gone forever.

That was how Mr. Sam Hall's pond was different. I had seen the sinners sink under the water, and watched them saved by the preacher's strong pull, coming back, every one living and singing.

Essie had told me my father was not coming home from the place he had gone. The only place I knew where nothing came back was the Blue Hole. So I decided to follow him down into the Blue Hole, falling until I caught up with his descent, then go on falling away from the August light forever. I was sitting by the Blue Hole, thinking these thoughts of sinking and falling, when Essie came up from the bushes alongside the creek and pulled me back to the house. She did not take me fishing again before I went to live in the city with my mother and her people, where I did not stay long. Alexander must know that my mother died soon after her husband, and I was taken in, when still a small child, by my father's mother and father. Sister finished college and settled in the house of our grandparents, which she has never left, which I never left until I set out on the road that led me, eventually, to the Occidental Hotel. Sister and I lived under the same roof for a long time. Negroes live in small houses on the road.

I think in the room with blue aqua wall-covering in the daylight hours, and sometimes after sunset, though there is no longer electricity in the rooms at night. Alexander wants to know what happened after I left Spring Ridge and before I arrived at the Occidental Hotel. I can recall some of it, a few fragments here and there, but not very much. The settled times are always harder to remember than the travelling time.

I did not marry, I did not have a family in an apartment high above the city streets. I knew a man who worked for a while in a newspaper's photographic archive, until he was fired for hiding away in the stacks and spending hours looking at images he was supposed to be filing. The pictures he was supposed to file were strange — the way they came from nowhere, went nowhere, meant nothing. Yet they were real things, he knew they were memories of things that had happened, drifting on the surface of time like things floating on the water of the Blue Hole, and he could not know what had happened, not from these photographs.

I have only fragments to show for the thinking of any one day, nothing more than fragments in my mind about settled life, nothing more than that. The scraps I show Alexander are like the photographs in the archive, fragments floating on the surface of an abyss without bottom, things that turn and drift and occasionally came close to touching, but do not cohere. When the weather turns cold this autumn, and the snows come to the mountains, and my fingers stiffen, I will stop trying to think, and that will be a good thing. I am telling you this because I cannot write, and you are listening because you cannot read, and that is how it is now between us.

You are listening because what I am telling you, what I am trying to explain, is about your father as well as my father, about extinctions that you must perform as certainly as I must perform them, about the woundings that always occur when the extinctions take place, the woundings that happen when one law is renounced and another law is embraced. If I could write and you could read, then you would understand what I am now telling you in my way of telling anything.

The morning I went alone to the Blue Hole, I thought of sinking and falling forever into the darkness. I would descend with the body of my father, inseparable from him and the South he came from. Then

Essie came up out of the bushes that lined the creek, prevented me from doing it, so my father was sinking without me. We went back up to the house on the green lawn.

That night, I thought more about descending into the Blue Hole. I told Mr. Penguin about it, but he could not hear and could not answer. I tried telling the mules in my father's barn about it, but they, I knew for a fact, could not answer.

Then I tried telling my thoughts to a rabbit that had starved to death in a hutch behind the white house after my father died, after my mother left for the city, after the household help (apart from Essie and the cook) departed, and no-one remained to mind the creature. And the rabbit replied:

The green corn moon is up, but the radiance is not strong enough for you to steal past Essie and make your way alone to the Blue Hole at midnight, and join your father in his falling. You have a story of peace, however — a script for peace, and a destination, and soon, very soon, you will write it, and join me in my dying, ending the starving and the explaining. Then, you will never again think of living without a father, or of Jupp and his dying in a box in Düsseldorf, and that will be a sinking and a sparing and an ending.

◡ 19

Though I did not return to the Blue Hole after the summer our father was murdered, I thought for days about catching up with him as he sank into darkness. Then I thought about it for months, then years, until I became a man and lived with a man with a remarkable knife and thought less and less about anything else. One summer midnight, I huddled under a bridge by a river in the city in the South. I thought once again about the only way to end the yearning thought of falling, and that was following my father in his sinking, going into that river and sinking into the darkness forever, as I had wanted to go into the Blue Hole when I was small.

Then, as I was studying the matter in the darkness, I saw an animal trotting in the muddy shadows of the bridge, and it was something that was not a dog and that was not a wolf, something that was in between. Curious, she circled me, and I was watching her circle me when the thought occurred to me that I need not follow my father down, if, instead, I followed the animal that was neither wolf nor dog, becoming, like it, impure.

I saw, high on the opposite bank of the river, brightly lit and glaring through the faint mist rising from the water, shining beside the bridge, the great billboard advertising the Occidental Hotel. A tattered picture of the hotel — the billboard was old — covered nearly all the spotlit expanse. It showed an oblong, flat-roofed block clad in frost-white glazed bricks and punctuated very regularly by square, frameless windows, its bulk gleaming like a low-lying cloud against a clear china-blue sky and a densely forested green hillside.

It was new, but I was old. The hotel did not smell. My father had smelled of the machine oil he used to lubricate the rifles stacked against a wall at the rear of the house at Spring Ridge. At the end of the afternoon, he smelled of the sweat he worked up in the cotton fields, because of the damp heat, not because he did much other than give Mr. Willis orders. He smelled of the machinery in the cotton gin, of his dogs, of cigar smoke, of the pulp adventure books stacked in the attic of my grandmother's house, books slowly disintegrating into dust, in which he had lost himself when a boy, he smelled of dry pulp and leather — all these manly smells, but all old, as old, it seemed to me, as I was. Long before my father was murdered, I was already as old as the world, already deep into the law of the old world, that of my father, of oil and leather and machinery and cotton lint, and that was the South he had come from.

The Occidental Hotel emblazoned on the billboard was very new and very white and clean, and I imagined it had no odour, no smells of tobacco and machine oil. It tempted me away from the darkness in the Blue Hole and the darkness that smelled of my father. I hesitated for a long hour. There was then the first letting go — it was only a little — and there was the grief of it, but the body of my father slipped away from me alone a little way toward the darkness, slid into the bottomless abyss, sinking into the river that was the Blue Hole, since the Blue Hole could be anywhere.

Many times after that midnight when I let my father go into the darkness, I wanted the calm and peace of the Blue Hole, but I could no longer imagine sinking with my father into it, now that I had let his body go a little way down without me, now that the thought of the Occidental Hotel had come into my mind. Wherever I travelled, after that midnight, I found pieces of the idea I had about the hotel I sought. I once saw a shiny black bar with wet rings left on it by chilled cocktail glasses, I once saw terrazzo floors in black and white geometrical patterns, and, somewhere, a room divider adorned with silhouettes of calypso dancers. I saw a Cadillac convertible dispense a woman in a black cocktail dress and a man in a narrow suit into a hotel entrance positioned under a porte-cochère shaped like a seashell. These things and places were not the Occidental Hotel, I knew that, but they were things that I imagined I would find there, if I ever found it at all.

20

The house of my father was white and wide, and it rose from a green lawn edged with tall trees. The Occidental Hotel had been white in the picture on the billboard, but by the time I reached it, years after seeing the billboard, the bleached, glassy bricks on the building's surface had been dimmed by sooty rain, and some had lost their glazed skins to freezing and thawing. The windows were as square and regular as they had been in the picture, and the structure's flat roofline still held straight and true against the china-blue sky and the green slope. But the immense parking lot was almost empty, and weeds had sprouted through fractures in its frost-heaved surface. The indoor Olympic pool had been drained, then filled up with dilapidated, faded canvas deck chairs. The scanty summer crowd, nearly the last guests to come here, had gone back to their homes in the city, and the congress of travelling folk had begun.

The travellers and I were the only guests that final autumn, after Mr. Steinway's scheme to market the resort to Japanese fall-foliage tourists came to nothing. But when the travelling folk were there, the zebra-striped Coconut Lounge and the huge Tamarack Dining Room bustled with sociable brio not witnessed at the Occidental since its Cold War heyday.

Dozens of people from neighbouring towns were employed for the first time in years, mixing drinks and serving meals again, turning down beds for flinty young travellers who were not interested in theory, taking turns emptying the ash trays of the travellers who lounged beside the dry Olympic pool, minding the elevators. The newspapers in nearby towns sent reporters to cover the event, since the Occidental had not been this busy in years, and editors toyed with readers' wishful thinking, never to be fulfilled, that this influx heralded a renaissance of the regional tourist industry.

The reporters from the local papers spent hours interviewing the travellers and writing up their interviews. Since they had never seen travellers before, and the only guests of the hotel in its prime had been settled people who did not interest them, the reporters very carefully wrote down what the travellers said and did.

At one point, two reporters at the same time interviewed a woman who had once owned several handbags made from the hides of animals whose species was threatened by extinction. She had otherwise done nothing noteworthy. Once, while desperate, she dipped into a famous book reputed to contain the key to placid living. The identity of the book does not matter, since each one of its sort tells the same story as all the rest. It does not matter, also, since she quickly stopped reading the book, after discovering she did not understand the rules it was asking her to follow. It does not matter which rules they were, since all rules, like printed dance steps put on the floor for students to follow, belong to the system, and the system was what dispirited her.

The woman who had owned several handbags mourned for a time, at least until she met and fell in love with a man of means who told her he could teach her to adore the system, any system. She did try to learn, especially after he assured her that he had learned the words of life by watching numerous television programs and motion pictures, and by understanding the famous book she had dipped into, then discarded.

But while they spooned up sundaes in a sleek stainless-steel diner one evening, the man of means broke off the affair, which had never been consummated, complaining that the woman was too clumsy to learn the rules and too obtuse to adore the system, any system — bitterly unfair accusations, I thought, since she had tried hard to learn and had made a little progress, and was only hindered by her birth under the law of the Cold War, which law she found incredible. So it was that the woman learned nothing about the words of life, or about any other certainties, and became a traveller, one of the travelling folk, who have no certain dwelling place on the earth, thereafter thinking of her ignorance in an appealing way.

Also among the travellers interviewed by curious reporters was an important child, let's call him Alexander, who had been, like every child when very young, a materialist. His hungers for food, for amusement, for distraction, for shelter were satisfied by watchful adults. He knew the want of nothing, and nothing he wanted was denied him. Until, that is, he wanted something that was unlawful for him to have. Failing to get it, Alexander experienced, for the first time in his short life, the fissure between the real and the ideal, and so became a Platonist. His parents and teachers then tried to convince him that the real, the empirically describable real, was all there was to know, but without success. So Alexander left his parents and teachers and found the travellers, then joined them in their wanderings and was reared by them. Little by little, he became as disreputable as they were, as the woman with several handbags was. Now he reads intently what I write in my room, and I write it for him.

⤳21

The hotel stands only five storeys tall, you would observe if you found it, but its lateral extent is vast on its sloping rural site. Shortly after the gathering of travelling folk adjourned, Mr. Steinway believed, wrecking crews from the city were to have arrived and stripped the public areas of the place of their furniture, flimsy faux-marble trim and wiry gilt wall-sconces, the expanses of terrazzo, the tangerine and blue plastic cut-outs of calypso dancers and palm trees on the lobby walls, even the Formica counter tops — everything salvageable and saleable or recyclable. But the destroyers did not come after a week had gone by, or a month. Indeed, they never came — perhaps because, contrary to Mr. Steinway's belief (and in confirmation of a widely held opinion), the owner did not in fact exist and therefore could not have given the order. So the ultra-modern décor remained exactly as it had been at the time of the Cuban missile crisis.

During that perilous October fortnight, President Kennedy faced the Soviet Union across the Atlantic Ocean and Neil Sedaka played the Tamarack Room for the fall-foliage tourists in from the city. The mood in the hotel, Mr. Steinway told me, was upbeat, as it always was, and no terror of imminent nuclear confrontation interrupted the happy dining hours. Freedom from fear was what the Occidental offered its clientele, after all, Mr. Steinway said — freedom from fear above all, communicated by the orchestration of sleek, modern appointments: the lava lamps in the lounges, the fantastical menu in the Tamarack Room, Sedaka's liquid voice, the streamlined architecture and festive decoration. Nothing really bad could happen at the Occidental, at this isolated refuge in the mountains (such was hotel's law, endlessly proclaimed by every employee, every detail of the decor), far from the teeming cities on the plain.

And in fact nothing troublesome did happen that October — and the dining and dancing at the Occidental, which never stopped even during the international emergency, went on for another few seasons, until the American idea of holidays in utopia shifted westward from the Southern mountains to Las Vegas, and the Occidental began its decline.

The owner, meanwhile, had begun to come up from the city to the hotel less and less frequently, and so it was that people eventually stopped asking for him or about him. He eventually stopped coming altogether, whereupon the running of the hotel fell entirely on Mr. Steinway's shoulders. At least that was the way Mr. Steinway remembered the sequence of events. Some denizens of nearby towns told another story. A young man, employed in the kitchen throughout the gathering of travellers, told me that nobody in those parts had believed in the existence of the owner since the time of the missile crisis, when he did not make a reassuring appearance to help steady nerves during the episode's most frightening hours. Even though everything at the hotel went on as usual, and Neil Sedaka sang, some frequent guests were scandalized by his absence at this crucial juncture in national history. The staff were bewildered.

All were rebuked by Mr. Steinway, who declared that he had received a telephone call from the owner as recently as last month, or perhaps it was last year, or perhaps he did not remember exactly. But it made no difference, he asserted: The owner had left clear instructions governing every aspect of the hotel's operation — instructions that Mr. Steinway vowed to carry out, and which he did obey, during and after the Cuban missile crisis, and down to the day I arrived, and the gathering of travellers broke up, and the hotel's doors closed for the last time. Thereafter, he found the quiet in the place distracting — or so he told Alexander and me during the evenings when we sat with him before the fire that burned in the enormous fieldstone fireplace in the lobby.

I spent my days, after the travellers checked out, wandering through the desolate public areas of the Occidental Hotel, which went on and on. I occasionally sat by the empty pool, occasionally walked around the parking lot. In the twilight hours, however, I watched the edge.

While doing so one evening, Alexander and I caught sight of what seemed at first to be a shadow passing quickly, like that of an aircraft. The unwary buck in the parking lot, scrawny from weeks in rut, did not bolt when the shadow broke out at the edge of the brilliantly red and yellow forest. But when he finally realized the coyotes were upon him, he twisted and tried to run away. They hurled their small bodies at his flanks, his throat. He stumbled and fell to the asphalt; they were upon him, ripping at his neck and head and gut. He died. Then the coyotes, yipping and quarrelling noisily among themselves, feasted on his carcass throughout the night.

When I next looked at the scene, shortly after dawn the following day, only one coyote, a yellowish-grey bitch, was still worrying and gnawing the bloody heap of entrails and skin.

I related the incident to Mr. Steinway, who was outraged that the bitch and her pack had managed to survive all the strychnine and thallium sulfate and Compound 1080 — advertised as "the most deadly, species-specific and foolproof predator poison in existence" — that he had carefully arrayed around the perimeter of the hotel grounds the summer before. A coyote kill in the parking lot should have been impossible, he thought. His war of extermination against the coyotes had been going on for years, after all, ever since the animals migrated into the mountain forests from the south-west and west, multiplied, ventured out of the woods, started eyeing players on the tennis courts and trotting in the shadows of joggers.

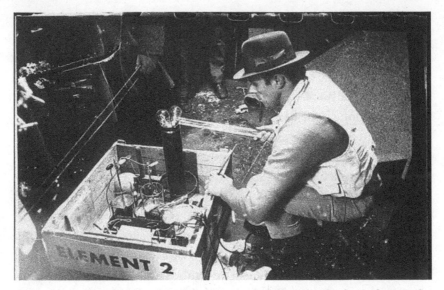

Figure 3: A photograph of Joseph Beuys taken by Ute Klophaus during the action entitled *Manresa*, 15 December 1966, Galerie Schmela, Düsseldorf. Collaborators included composer Henning Christiansen and sculptor Bjørn Nørgaard. A box, "Element 2," from which Beuys extracts objects—pieces of electrical equipment, a paper disc, a toy bird attached to a stick, a plate decorated with a Crucifixion tableau, and other props—that he then variously manipulates (the bird flaps its wings, other things are merely carried) in the space between "Element 2" and "Element 1."

"Element 1:" Leaning against the wall, outside the frame of Klophaus' picture, half a wooden Greek cross wrapped in felt.

From time to time, Beuys shouts out the sentence: "Where is Element 3?"

There are two bottles, one made of lead, the other filled with milk. Beuys drinks from the milk bottle. There is a copper herder's (or pilgrim's) staff, or crozier.

"Beuys set out as a wanderer with the crozier," writes Friedhelm Mennekes in an extended meditation on this performance. "Again and again he had himself photographed as a guide of stags, as a nomad, as a demonstrator in the desert of Western society, as one always in

search of the economic, spiritual and cultural energies lost. This search is practice, is sculpture. It is at the same time a departure and an escape from old securities."

Though he used items from Christian iconography throughout his career — notably the cross, drawn or painted or sculpted, Beuys was not a Christian in any traditional sense. Christ, for him, as for his mentor Rudolf Steiner, meant primordial creativity, the transcendent, the occult Logos — not the Palestinian Jew, the concrete, mortal Jesus of orthodox theology. It is with Steiner's inflection that Beuys speaks when he tells Mennekes that "the form in which the personification of Christ manifests itself in our day is the element of movement itself. The person who is moving."

In 1522, the convalescent Basque adventurer Ignacio de Loyola came to the Catalan town of Manresa, and embarked on a year-long season of intense prayer attended by profound, often suicidal depression. St. Ignatius' famous Spiritual Exercises were conceived at Manresa. Like other commentators on Beuys' performance, Mennekes draws a line between Ignatius' desolation and the artist's deep crisis in the mid-1950s, through which spiritual and psychological disarray Beuys discovered his true vocation, which was his original vocation, to be an artist of a certain sort. A thaumaturge; a healer of modernity's discontents and alienations; a homeopath who will handle ordinary materials — iron, fat, felt, cardboard, a copper pilgrim's staff, milk, lead — in the course of symbolic rituals or performances. For Mennekes and for a great many of Beuys' disciples, every prop and gesture means something. Thus, the half-cross "hints at the political divisions between East and West, at the artificial separation of cultures and populations." By drawing on the wall the missing half of the cross, Beuys heralds "the task of reuniting Europe and Asia."

"Then he goes back to the box and takes a disc of cardboard out of it, puts it with a piece of string round his neck on his back and goes back to Element 1. *He symbolically carries the circle as a sign of the wholeness of the two divided parts [of the cross]. Finally, there is a plate with a model of Christ on the cross. He carries it to the same spot* to suggest that the divided can only be put together with pain, sacrifice and the risk of death." When Beuys drinks the milk, "he draws vital energy from nature in order to transform it into practical action."

Note the ordinariness, the anti-art crudity and humility, of the objects — the cardboard disc, the souvenir plate, milk, and so on — that are said to express Beuys' thinking in the ritual drama of Manresa. In Sade Fourier Loyola, *Roland Barthes remarks on the efforts of the Jesuits to establish a reputation for St. Ignatius' Exercises as "laboured," "literarily impoverished," the opposite of the "fine writing" that the saint's religious order did so much to encourage in Europe and abroad. "Here," Barthes says, "we find once more the old modern myth according to which language is merely the docile and insignificant instrument for the serious things that occur in the spirit, the heart or the soul. The myth is not innocent; discrediting the form serves to exalt the importance of the content: to say:* I write badly *means:* I think well."

22

On this unseasonably warm winter evening in 1956, Jupp crouches within the box he ordered from Kleve, remembering no pleasure. So remember for him a time when he was innocent, a youth in Germany before the war, before the idea of being an artist had occurred to him, long before he achieved the fame that would make him the prey of biographers.

Remember, because Jupp cannot, the early summer of 1936, when the gruelling drills and incessant competitions of the Hitler Youth, the cross-country marches and camping expeditions, delighted him, when he and his comrades lusted after news about the upcoming Olympic games in Berlin, when there were many stirrings in the alleys and laneways of his brain, though none of these could be properly called thoughts. Each boy talked jubilantly about the German star athletes who, none doubted, would harvest the most medals. They speculated about the new technology they had heard about, *far-seeing* in German, television, radio with flickering pictures, like talkies, but unlike talkies inasmuch as the capture and far-off presentation of the discus throw or high jump would take place, by a miracle wrought by German science, simultaneously. The Olympics, the papers said, were to be broadcast live via television to salons in Berlin and Hamburg. Basing their fantasies on illustrations in popular magazines, the boys imagined visually hissing, tiny, fiercely radiant electric screens in thickly curtained rooms, where each boy who could not win admission to the stadium itself wanted to be.

Jupp had just turned fifteen. He was taller than he had been at fourteen, still a virgin and not yet in a hurry to terminate his stainlessness. Hitler Youth activities ate deeper into each day and evening than they had before 1936, but he did not care, since school meant less and less to him as the term dragged to an end. Jupp tolerated the ideological instruction he was given on some Wednesday nights (though it was too much like school for his taste), because enduring it was the price he paid for fellowship in Kleve's Hitler Youth unit, where he could pound, or be pounded by, another slender boy in the boxing ring, where he could aim and shoot his assigned Browning rifle on the firing range, and bivouac with his unit close to the Dutch border, gaming at combat with Germany's ancient enemies.

He was not an ideologue, though the ideology had seeped into his brain's citadel, and he was easily compliant with the regime of knowledge within which he lived. He could have been a leader, had he been as patient with disciples as he would later become, when he was famous, but he was not patient then. His desires were reckless, eager but not especially curious, and directed, for the most part, toward getting and keeping physical eminence among the comrades, his peers.

These close acquaintances, decades later, will remember Jupp at fifteen as a lackadaisical high school student, an enthusiast for the sports he played, but one without a sports fanatic's knack for keeping scores and records exactly straight in his head. They will contradict what he himself recalled about his youth, that it was a period when he was keenly interested in scientific topics, saying about him that the only things that appealed to him were his gun, boxing, camp-craft, the exercise of his limbs. He read the authors on the official syllabus, but none beyond. Perhaps offended or distracted by his subsequent celebrity, not inclined to take him seriously in any case (perhaps because thousands of people in the great world did), the acquaintances will have forgotten, if they ever knew, what happened to Jupp in the late spring of 1936, changing him.

It started at the end of an ideological training session, one intended (as most were) to dignify the cult of the Führer, having to do with the sixteen Nazi martyrs who fell in Munich during Hitler's insurrection in 1923. The pack leader, Horst, a man of 24 with close-cropped, obedient sand-coloured hair smartly parted on the side, announced that a new directive had come down from Hitler Youth headquarters in Berlin. From now until the end of the summer, Horst said, the men in the unit would be scattering themselves across fields and waste places around Kleve, collecting wild plants for use at the Rudolf-Hess Hospital in Dresden, where homeopathic medical experiments were underway. He went on to say that a list of plants to be collected would be forthcoming, and that the expeditions were to begin immediately.

But Horst, how are we to know what to look for? an obscure lad of about fourteen, new to the Hitler Youth, asked.

You probably know some already, Horst replied. The others, Herr Fröhlingsdorf will show you how to identify. He'll be here next week.

And, true to Horst's word, Michael Fröhlingsdorf came to the meeting of the boys a week later, bringing detailed colour plates of the plants to be gathered for the experimental treatment, with tisanes and medicinal drops and lozenges, of the Third Reich's ailing and dying.

23

All the boys knew that Herr Fröhlingsdorf taught biology and racial science at the high-school, and was regarded by their parents as something of a notable in little Kleve, because, though not much over thirty, he had already written several booklets about biology and National Socialism for Eher Verlag, the Nazi publishing house, tracts that they, the parents, said they did not understand.

The townsfolk also liked his transparently blonde, formidably Nazi wife, Ingvild, who, they said among themselves, would be a perfect German woman were she to bear Herr Fröhlingsdorf a houseful of children. For his part, Michael Fröhlingsdorf was narrow, lean, with a trunk perhaps too long, as if his spine had been stretched at birth. He had unruly hair the colour and texture of dry autumn hay, plain and autocratic and somewhat owlish good looks, a stoop and the faintest beginnings of a paunch, and an unspotted pedigree that, genealogists had demonstrated, could be traced back, on both sides, to sturdy Aryan couples busily procreating in Hesse during the 1730s.

For the week after Horst's announcement of the herb-gathering scheme, Jupp quietly dreaded the appearance of Michael Fröhlingsdorf at the forthcoming Hitler Youth meeting. He very much liked hiking and tenting in the woods, but he knew how to identify only the commonest weeds, and did not want to learn how to find others. Unlike most of his youth group's other activities, this one promised to be tiresome.

He hated the boredom of school and his life at home, but at least he had been able to escape it on Hitler Youth excursions. Now that route, it seemed, would be closed to him, at least temporarily, because Herr Fröhlingsdorf and the Hitler Youth hierarchs were about to turn the camaraderie he liked into something that resembled school. Surely, he thought, traipsing through pastures, avoiding a step, ankle-deep, into cow flop, in search of weeds suitable for harvest, would bore him exquisitely.

Neither Herr Fröhlingsdorf's initial presentation, nor the group's first sally into the pastures, disappointed Jupp. He dutifully collected the plants he had learned to recognize, or knew already, but joylessly, even after Horst's exhortations to maximum effort on behalf of sick racial comrades and the advance of German science. Jupp longed to get back into the boxing ring, or back into paramilitary manoeuvring in the countryside, where at least he excelled at something.

Jupp was further dismayed, a couple of weeks after the harvesting had begun, when Herr Fröhlingsdorf turned up at another Wednesday evening meeting of Kleve's Hitler Youth. Horst announced that he had invited the teacher to return after he, the teacher, expressed his interest in addressing the boys and youths a second time.

To Jupp's surprise — he was not accustomed to hearing such things from teachers — Herr Fröhlingsdorf began with an apology to the youths. It had occurred to him, he said, that the first time he talked to the troops, he probably dwelt over-long on the technical identification of the plants to be gathered for the hospital. It is well to know such things, he continued, so that the forests and fields do not remain merely anonymous, blank greenesses. But, he went on, he had not said nearly enough about *why* these particular plants were on the list from Berlin — and this omission meant that the boys had been dispatched on their errand without correct preparation.

He produced from the leather satchel he always carried a coloured lithograph of a plant with sunburst yellow blossoms and pale, stemless green-blue leaves. All the boys recognized it immediately, from the previous instruction. It was a picture of St. John's wort, one of the items on the list sent down from Berlin.

Then Herr Fröhlingsdorf commenced speaking, not about the detailed physical traits that had tired Jupp the last time, but rather about what he called the exciting renewal of German medicine then underway in places such as the Rudolf-Hess hospital and some re-education camps — how the lore of herbs was being rescued from the oblivion to which "enlightened" science had consigned it in the nineteenth century, and brought back into the good work of healing the sick.

St. John's wort, for instance, was not merely the invasive weed it was sometimes made out to be. The old Europeans knew better, they revered the plant, and even told children given to bashing through its habitat that anyone who carelessly crushed the herb underfoot was liable to be trampled to death by faerie horses. Legends of its power had been preserved in the genus name — *Hypericum,* from the Greek *hyper* (above) and *eikon* (image, picture) — which might refer to the peasant custom, from time out of mind, of stringing up the flowering stalk over sacred images on St. John's Day, June 24, as prophylaxis against untimely death, specters and lightning strikes.

The shrub belonged to the sun, Herr Fröhlingsdorf' said. According to the old herbals, it incarnated the dark-dispelling resplendence of the Nordic light-god, Baldur, hence the traditional prescription of its blood-red oil as a specific against insanity, and its popularity among Crusaders as an all-heal. Baldur's magic was being tested in Dresden, he said, by doctors who were investigating the beneficial properties of St. John's wort in cases of, among other maladies, depression. He pronounced himself certain that the herb's effectiveness would be confirmed, its ancient high reputation vindicated. The knowledge that had been passed along, down to the dawn of modernist amnesia, by tale-tellers of gods and heroes, alchemists and healers, far wiser about the human condition than materialistic modern medics, would then take its rightful place, he said, in the beneficial armoury of the new German science.

Herr Fröhlingsdorf then went down the list of plants the boys were to harvest, pausing at each item to recount the folklore, cosmological and healing myth and saga, occult tradition, and current medical speculation that pertained to it.

Despite his well-tended indifference (verging on hostility) to learning of any sort, Jupp was intrigued by the cabinet of curiosities Herr Fröhlingsdorf' had opened wide. Yet the part about Baldur and light and wort's crimson oil disturbed something in him, his complacent anti-intellectualism perhaps, and he sensed in himself a gentle motion he had not experienced for a few years, at least since he was a boy turning into a youth, when he forsook the loneliness of his childhood and discovered the rough team sports and marches and comradeship of the German Youngfolk.

As if hearing the melancholy folk-tunes of a country from which he had been exiled long before, Jupp listened intently to the teacher's talk of gods and influential planets, the secret virtues of plants that, if he knew their names at all, had meant nothing to him before that night. As the presentation wore on, he felt a longing quicken inside him. It was a desire that did not yet know its object, a discontenting hunger that did not know what could satisfy it. But he had felt this keen unrest with ordinary reality years before, as a small boy, when his mother recited to him the tales of Sigurd the Dragon Slayer, when he saw, in books he could not yet read, plates of Josef Hoffman's quivering, dithyrambic stage-sets for *Das Rheingold,* when he heard, from the flaring horn of the wind-up record player in his parents' living room, the farewell song of the swan prince in *Lohengrin,* who could join himself only to a woman who did not ask his name.

~24

In that summer of 1936, Jupp began to beg off from after-school outings and sports practices with a variety of lies, sometimes having to do with chores his parents allegedly expected him to do at home or at the flour and feed store where his father worked, sometimes with the homework that had (also allegedly) become important to him. Jupp's slacking was almost unnoticeable at first. It was sensed by his comrades as merely a new unavailability to do the things everyone knew he enjoyed doing, such as boxing and shooting and cross-country hiking. Horst noticed that Jupp was more distracted than usual, suspected a girl was involved, decided to say nothing for the time being.

But then, around mid-summer, Jupp became, in Horst's view, more remote than he had been—so the young man asked Jupp if anything were troubling him. No, Jupp replied, lying—just duties at the flour store and the last bit of homework before the summer break. Horst was not convinced by Jupp's answer, but let the matter drop without further comment. Horst did not know—no-one did—that Jupp, by this time, was slipping via the long, more obscure way around to the town library, keeping out of sight as much as possible.

This activity had started nervously, after Herr Fröhlingsdorf's second presentation, with Jupp's sidling into the library, where he never went, and asking for the location of books on plants. Can you be more precise? the librarian, a florid, untidy woman wearing a tight skirt too long for the season, glancing up, whispered sharply back at the boy. Flowers, Jupp said, suddenly menaced, I'm looking for books about German flowers. The librarian thought Jupp was about to bolt through the door, so she quickly said: Thomé, Otto Wilhelm. *Flora of Germany, Austria and Switzerland.* Reference shelves. Here, I'll show you where it is.

Leafing through the 1905 edition of Professor Thomé's stout work, Jupp was quickly disappointed. There was much technical description about plant morphology and taxonomy, which did not interest him, and many coloured pictures of splayed plants and plant parts with Latin nomenclature inscribed in copperplate on each print alongside the common German name, printed in *Fraktur.* He had wanted, or thought he wanted, stories like those the teacher had told, snippets of lore, legends — and none were here.

Then, just as he was about to shut the book and return home, Jupp flipped past, then turned back to, a plate that depicted the grey green leaves and purplish-black fruit, white flowers and prickly stems of blackthorn (*Prunus spinosa*), a shrub he knew. He remembered the dense hedge-rows he and his Hitler Youth comrades skirted or hid behind when they manoeuvred through the fields around Kleve. He remembered falling into a cresting white wave of blackthorn blossoms while playing a war game, how the coarse spines beneath the froth painfully snatched at his face and arms, how the other lads, laughing, pulled him out, and he and they resumed the tracking of unfriendlies. Blackthorn, for Jupp, was common, impenetrable and spiny (hence to be avoided when running across pastures), and the tart sloes, even when mellowed by autumn's first frost, puckered his mouth.

He studied the images on the coloured lithograph for a long moment, then realized that, for reasons not yet known to him, he wanted to possess it — not the fruit or flower illustrated, but the plate itself. Had he been able to say so, he might have remarked that here the blackthorn was perfected, painless, eternal, like art, stories of Sigurd, the music of *Lohengrin* — not like the living, menacing shrubs he encountered on the edge of pastures, where farmers planted them to keep livestock in or out, where they blocked Jupp's way forward.

In an instant, almost simultaneously, greedy options flickered across his mind. He could open his knife, slice out the page, steal it; then it would be his. But were he to be caught, he would be disgraced in front of the other boys, punished at home, perhaps turned over to the police. Or he could buy a copy of it, but he did not know where to find one. And even if he knew where, he did not have the money to buy something that would surely be expensive. Or he could copy it. Jupp had never attempted, since he was a child, to copy a picture. Now he wanted to attempt it. He thought about it for a long minute. Copying the plate, he told himself, would be like boxing — something tried, failed, tried again until it happened, and then he would be boxing, or copying, and possessing.

The next day, after school, Jupp bought pencils, crayons and a stack of typewriter paper at the stationery shop in Adolf-Hitler-Strasse and went back to the library, where he made his first copy of Thomé's pictures of the blackthorn's parts, and then another attempt. Jupp's laborious sloes looked like eggs, or the pendulous testicles of rams, not fruit, he thought, so he laid down another sheet of paper and tried again. A few days and numerous drawings later, Jupp succeeded in doing a cautious, pedantic copy of the blackthorn illustration, or a fraction of it. That he had managed to do this surprised and pleased him, even if his hand could not reproduce exactly the professor's antiseptically pristine line.

Throughout the summer of 1936, as holidays ended and school resumed, as the Olympics came and went and the other boys talked of nothing else, Jupp sneaked into the library whenever the demands of the Hitler Youth allowed, and copied. He copied botanical illustrations from Thomé, then those from other authors whose books he discovered on the same shelf, until, as the autumn came on, he copied better, by which I mean that his drawing was an increasingly obedient rendering of the original that he found beauty in, and that he thought was art. One day, having grown confident about copying, and tired of it, and having decided he wanted to try something other than what he had become good at, he began to wonder what drawing the real plant, the real tree, the real leaf would be like. So he studied art books to find out what landscapes were supposed to be, then bought a sketchbook at the stationery store, and went into the Lower Rhineland forests and fields, drawing there. No-one must know, he told himself. He was taking a risk. He knew the leaders in the Hitler Youth discouraged solitary hiking by adolescents on the grounds that it was too much like the wandering, idling indulged in by the bourgeoisie — connoisseurship of nature, instead of vigorous preparation for biological soldiering.

He went anyway, after school when he could, and on Sundays. The small plants Jupp did not have time to delineate in the field, he clipped and brought home to draw, after which he mounted and labelled each vegetable fragment on a wide sheet of buff paper obtained from the butcher in Dinnendahlstrasse. He transcribed notes on each plant into his sketchbook from the botanical manuals and field guides he found in the library. In this way, Jupp's sketchbooks and packages of typewriter paper, one after another, filled up with notes, with copies, with drawings of living flowers as long as they bloomed, of trees until they went naked and then of the bones of trees in their nakedness.

The sketches of plants and, later, of the landscape, described the topic exactly as he had witnessed it laid out in art books. He refrained from interpreting the motif in any way not authorized by the sunlit, shadowless scientific illustrations that he copied. A decade would pass, the war would be over, Jupp would have entered art school, before his drawing became more intimate than dictation, before his hand allowed itself to express, rather than mimic, the quiddity, the significant form, of the thing it portrayed. But now he drew constantly as he had learned to do from looking at books, copying from herbals and botanies in the library at those times in 1936 and early 1937 when he was prevented from drawing in the fields by weather or school or the Hitler Youth or mandatory presence at the festivities of the Party's holy days, or the winter disappearance of the blooms.

This was the new life he wanted to keep secret from everyone: from his comrades and Horst, because they would think his obsession absurd, perhaps unmanly; and from his parents as much as possible, who already suspected his long absences from home, which he felt no compunction to explain, were not prompted by schoolwork or Hitler Youth commitments. The parents would object to anything that might distract Jupp from the career they had mapped out for him, at a fat-wrapping machine in Kleve's mammoth margarine factory. And throughout that fall and winter, he kept his secret even from Michael Fröhlingsdorf, whose biology student he had become in the late summer of 1936, and whom he now loved.

25

Because Kleve was a small provincial town, without a university library, Herr Fröhlingsdorf owned the books he needed for teaching and for his ideological writing on race and science. His collection of reference works, field guides, journals and the rare illustrated botanies he bought from an antiquarian book dealer in Düsseldorf had long ago overflowed the study in the modest flat in Kleve's old town he shared with his wife Ingvild, and surged into the living room, the dining room, into the couple's bedroom. He had a rough sense of where everything was in this clutter, or thought he had, until a thundery afternoon in the early spring of 1937 when he reached for Bronn's 1860 translation of *On the Origin of Species* — which bore the grandiloquently essayistic German title *On the Origin of Species in the Animal and Plant Kingdom through Natural Selection, or the Preservation of Perfected Races in the Struggle for Existence* — and did not find it.

He had failed to return it to its customary spot, or loaned it to someone — he did not know which, but he now wanted to check his usually acute memory of a passage, needed for quotation in a lecture on racial hygiene, against the printed text of Bronn's Darwin. He rummaged for a moment among the volumes and magazines stacked on the desk in his study, did not find it, decided to waste no more time looking for it, to seek it, instead, in the one place in Kleve where a copy might exist, the town library, which he rarely used.

Coming into the ponderously becolumned *Gründerzeit* building out of the cold spring rain, Herr Fröhlingsdorf quickly located the book he was looking for, checked the passage—he had indeed remembered it exactly—and was about to head back out through the foul weather to his flat and desk and typewriter when he caught sight of Jupp, crouched over a book propped open on a table littered with sheets of paper.

Finding another of his students, one of the bright ones, studying in the library on a stormy afternoon would hardly have surprised Michael Fröhlingsdorf, but finding Jupp there, sharply concentrating on the book before him, made the teacher curious. Like the boy's other high school instructors, he thought Jupp to be listless, uninterested in school, possibly even a little slow, certainly keen on nothing that required intellectual effort. True, Jupp's marks in biology that term had been marginally better than those in his other courses. Yet still, even here, in what appeared to be his favourite class, he lagged behind the others, seemed to be dreaming even more soddenly and abstractly than other youths. Perhaps he has finally decided to get down to work, thought Herr Fröhlingsdorf, who resolved to say hello.

For a panicked instant, seeing the teacher crossing the room in his direction, Jupp thought the only way to avoid calamity would be to hide the wretched scrawlings that lay on the table by the book of plant illustrations. But there was no time, no place to conceal them. The pugnacious nerve, the young male bravado, that served him well in the boxing ring deserted him. He wanted to escape; he could not. He stood up, as one should in the presence of a teacher. Herr Fröhlingsdorf now stood beside the table, greeted him with the usual formality, politely asked if he might see what Jupp was doing in the library on this afternoon of thundery showers.

26

In dumb turmoil — the surprised, stupid sensation that earthworms must feel in their simple guts when spaded up from eternal night underground into the sunshine — Jupp walked home from the library and retreated at once to his neat room.

His teacher wants to see everything, Jupp thought wordlessly, like an earthworm. Everything — the notebooks and sketchbooks, the loose sheets of drawings heaped up in Jupp's cupboard, the pressed specimens taped to oblongs of butcher's paper. He was afraid of something, he did not know what. Disapproval? His teachers had always disapproved of him, chided him to work harder, and he had ignored them as much as possible, ascribing their complaints, when he felt the need to ascribe them to anything, to the bourgeois, old-style consciousness still deep-rooted in high school teachers. despite the national revolution.

But Herr Fröhlingsdorf was not, Jupp thought, a teacher of that sort. Though as authoritarian and aloof as any other teacher Jupp had, he spoke in his lectures and demonstrations of the organic wholeness of nature, the cosmic energies that course through all living things that are good and wholesome, binding them into sublime unities driven to survive and thrive, until decadence overtakes them. He talked in this exalted way even when explaining textbook illustrations of an oak leaf's epidermis, mesophyll, stomata. He knew things. He had taught the herb-gathering Hitler Youth to recognize, then ignore, *Cytisus scoparius,* common broom. You don't need to harvest it, he said, because broom contains alkaloids that afflict the heart—though it flowers beautifully after the hottest days of summer, and, however toxic it might be, it possesses the distinction of having lent its demotic name, *planta genista*, to a royal house of Europe. So while it did not serve the lads' immediate purposes, he said, broom was interesting, deserving attention (since it might have health-giving properties nobody had yet guessed), and certainly no ordinary weed. On his solitary walks during late summer's hot days, Jupp found broom on forsaken land, scissored off its staves of golden yellow blooms, drew them as carefully as he could, mounted the pressed and dried flowers in his herbarium—which now, in the spring of 1937, Herr Fröhlingsdorf wanted to see.

He will not approve, thought Jupp for a long while, without any elevation of the animal dread into words and syntax. A sickly, yellowish stench, like that of fever, settled in the shadowed basement of his boy's body. Then, as he pondered the matter, something like anger began gradually to dispel the thick, repulsive fearfulness—controlled, strategic, cleansing anger rising against the earthworm's fear of sunshine, shouldering it aside.

⌢27

Three days later, having made an appointment to see his teacher after school, Jupp hauled in his things in rucksacks and cloth bags, and unpacked them on Herr Fröhlingsdorf 's demonstration table. the fat stack of wide brown pages, to each of which was affixed a fragile, dried vegetable specimen harvested in the neighbourhood of Kleve, the loose sheets, the sketchbooks filled with notations and pencil and crayon drawings (copied from books or rendered from nature) of blooms, leaves, trees, shrubs. The teacher dismantled Jupp's pile, distributed its elements on the table in the dusty, wood-panelled biology room warmed by an obese iron stove, then began to ponder the pages that lay before him.

Jupp watched in silence as the teacher slowly turned a page, dropped his hand into his lap while he studied what was in front of him — the individual specimen, the drawing, the inscription — then raised his hand to turn another.

After what seemed to Jupp like a cruel, barren suspense of time — all of it passed with hardly a murmur from the teacher, no hint of praise or blame — Herr Fröhlingsdorf quietly closed Jupp's last notebook, pushed his chair back from the table, and declared himself pleased by most of what he had seen.

He had a few questions, which Jupp answered, about the length of time Jupp had been at this work, about his sources, the illustrated manuals he had consulted. He suggested lines of research Jupp might pursue, especially in the field of botanical illustration. Jupp, he went on, must try to find the superb flowers of Pierre-Joseph Redouté, who flourished as an illustrator under both the *ancien régime* and Robespierre, during the time of Napoleon, under both Bourbon restorations, and the July Monarchy — a textbook case, the teacher said, one not to be emulated, of remarkable talent in misalliance with typically French political opportunism.

Herr Fröhlingsdorf then mentioned the anatomical vagueness of Jupp's trees and shrubs, a fault that could be overcome, he continued, by slowing down and imitating Caspar David Friedrich, whose oaks and conifers were always excellent, correct. But he admired the herbarium made of butcher's paper — he invited Jupp to show it to the class — and he liked, on the whole, Jupp's cautious, economical renderings of the blossoms and branches and body-parts he had found in books. He thought Jupp's drawings from nature showed promise, as he put it, and would improve with closely attentive practice, with more excursions to where the flowers were about to bloom under cloudy spring skies.

Jupp, he said, copied well, without the injection of personal opinion, and, like Thomé himself, with due, anti-decadent reverence for the visible, sunlit appearance of the thing in front of him. Jupp should remember that exacting depiction of the motif was the gift to visual art of the scientific Nordic mind, such as Leonardo's. In language I approve, after my own close examination of the subject, of art, especially modern French art, which is depraved, he told Jupp that impressions, vaporings, insinuations, finesse, generalities in art were vicious, symptoms of foreign, especially French, disorder and moral derangement. He liked best Jupp's transcriptions of Thomé's illustrations, which he encouraged Jupp to imitate always.

The teacher praised in Jupp's drawings, that is, the facticity, the exclusive fidelity to retinal truth, that the artist whom Jupp is to become will never wholly unlearn, discard after the war. Then, ten years after 1937, his hand will move more freely, but will still know reverence, will faithfully describe the shape of mind caressing the sensuous contours of the real, as Dürer's did. He will always depict frankly, never paraphrase, never let his art decline into soulless abstraction or narcotic materialism. It will always generate a politics that is German, radical, monumental, free of contamination by elements alien to the race, protective of the earth.

You know from your training, Herr Fröhlingsdorf said, speaking, as he often did, of the soul, that hiking alone is bad for the soul, that lonely pursuits can lead to a decay in one's feelings of oneness with the racial community. It's bourgeois, this solitary communing with Nature, and we reject it. But nothing's wrong with the kind of scrutiny you've embarked on here, if guided by the national community's feelings and needs. You should stop going out on your own. It's not healthy. I need to do some observation of Lower Rhineland flora for a handbook I'm co-authoring, and I could use an assistant who knows the local plants and can draw a little. Why don't you come along?

Jupp blinked once, then said: Where do you want to go?

You know that better than I do, Herr Fröhlingsdorf replied. I'm not familiar with this part of Germany, you've lived here all your life, and Horst tells me you are good at reading maps. You can lead us to the habitats of all the plants on my list, since, from the looks of your herbarium, you've obviously been scouting out the neighbourhood for some time. A good man, Horst — he says you like being outside, and both he and I think that all the time you've been spending in the library probably isn't a good use of your time. So what do you think?

Jupp sensed benign conspiracy, and liked what he sensed: So Herr Fröhlingsdorf and Horst had talked about him, noted his slackening of interest in the manly activities of the Hitler Youth. What else did they say? Jupp had enjoyed his solitary walks, more than he had expected to. He had enjoyed the desire of drawing, it had quickened him, and that desire had linked Horst to Herr Fröhlingsdorf, and now was linking him, Jupp, to Herr Fröhlingsdorf in the chain of desiring that the drawing had created, nourished, occasioned.

Jupp said aloud: Yes, I think I would like that.

You'll draw or take cuttings or do whatever you like, and I'll collect specimens, the teacher said. Talk to Horst and your parents about it. I don't want this to distract you from your responsibilities, especially your schoolwork. But it's field study I have to do, and I would like to have you along.

Herr Fröhlingsdorf concluded the session by giving Jupp a signed copy of his recently published tract, *Darwin and the Failure of Jewish Science*.

~**28**

Remember Jupp's excited homeward walk after his interview with the teacher, remember that he was hardly slowed by knapsacks and bags full of drawings and notebooks, through scanty, cold drizzle to Tiergartenstrasse, his quicker pace into his room at the back of the apartment, where he read *Darwin* until the dinner hour. He went there again after dinner, when his father switched on the radio and began to drink, and plotted the routes of his and his teacher's future excursions on a finely detailed topographical and political map of the Lower Rhineland and adjacent districts of the Netherlands. It was the map he had learned to read, in the previous spring, while playing combat games near the Dutch border with his Hitler Youth detachment.

Three years later, after the German invasion of the low countries in May, 1940, he will listen intently to radio bulletins from the front, and sense exultant mastery in himself because he will already know from his intensive map-reading classes the name of each town and village German troops and tanks thunder through, and how the low Dutch land lies in the path of what will be said, on Reich radio, is a heavily resisted but inexorable advance.

But three years before, in the spring of 1937, Jupp understood the syntax in the map's spangle of blue and black lines, dots and symbols laid down on coloured expanses. He had used, and continued to use, this knowledge to plan the overrunning of defenses raised by teams of other Hitler Youth posing as enemies, to circumvent their positions, to recapture the hamlets, farms and stream-crossings they had occupied. Now the map lay open before him on his desk, and he imagined the trails and forest pathways he saw there as routes to another knowledge, of Michael Fröhlingsdorf, who had loomed over the library table on a stormy afternoon and who loomed, tall and serious and slender, in Jupp's new imaginations of what men were, how they moved on the earth, what they thought.

Before he heard the teacher talk to the Hitler Youth on the lore and science of herbs, he had learned about grown men from Karl May's novels about Old Shatterhand, set on an American frontier May had never seen and that he invented for his male characters to show bravery and loyalty in. Jupp had also learned, crucially, from the older Hitler Youth boys and young men with whom he trained and played. Especially, there was Horst, who taught Jupp to box valiantly, to hate ideas and persons worthy of correct hatred, to march long distances without complaint, to dead-eye a distant paper target with the Browning, to be hard, active, impassive. These young men close to Jupp were vowed, publically at least, to plain toughness and indifference to schooling and to suffering, their own and that of others. The leaders enforced strict discipline among the boys, they instilled, by word and example, in the boys the conviction that to be German and male was to be natively excellent, above guilt or blame, driven by the animal instincts to father, fight, dominate.

They, and all propaganda instruments at the disposal of Party and state, constantly proposed to Jupp and the other youths this idea of masculinity. Nobody he knew in Kleve ever questioned or opposed the idea. The newspapers, the teachers, the townsfolk said that those who showed contempt for the idea had already been confined to concentration camps or had fled abroad, where they could contaminate only others of their kind. And that is why, Jupp thought (if he ever thought about the matter at all), he knew no-one with another idea about being male, except his father.

Each evening, Joseph came home tired from the flour and fodder store he operated with his brother, ate, in sullen quietude, the dinner his wife put before him, listened to speeches and dainty, vapid music that bleated from his Strength Through Joy radio set after dinner, while sipping beer, until he dozed off. Joseph had joined the Party after January 30, 1933, when everybody was signing on. But he had no enthusiasm for politics, beyond a desire not to be hurt, so he was not particularly pleased or proud when, in 1933, his twelve-year-old son announced his eagerness to join a march with Kleve's German Youngfolk. Jüppken, Catholics do not do such things, Jupp's mother told the boy, while his father sipped beer and said nothing. His mother objected only a little, only quietly, and soon grew tired of what objecting she did, since the streets had become quiet since the Nazis took control, and, anyway, all the other mothers were letting their boys march.

So he marched, ending a childhood spent mostly in schoolrooms he felt nothing for and at home, playing solitary games with his toys, bored and lonesome but not especially introspective, a childhood that had been most nearly happy when he listened to his mother's Wagner recordings, or travelled mentally through the storybook places his mother's tale-telling took him to, or wandered alone, mostly inattentively, through the town park. Jupp marched out of his apartment and joined the boys he knew from school and playground, becoming more than a child. Joseph drank beer while listening to the radio, became more and more ignorable with the passage of seasons, like a stain in the living-room carpet that people used to notice, then became accustomed to, finally forgot about. In 1937, Jupp's mother Maria went to Mass every Sunday, read the new German translation of *Gone With the Wind* in the evenings, hoped Jupp would someday be hired at the margarine factory, thought about him when he brought home worryingly inferior reports from school, but even then only long enough to scold him a little.

In any case, by the spring of 1937, whatever need for parents Jupp had ever felt, beyond the practical supply of food and shelter, disappeared. The lad did not need a father to show him what men were. He had a hero.

Figure 4: A photograph taken during the Action entitled *I like America and America Likes Me*, performed by Joseph Beuys and a coyote at the René Block Gallery, New York, May, 1974. Copies of *The Wall Street Journal* were placed on the floor, and the coyote with which Beuys lived for three days urinated on them. A recording of turbine noises played on an audio system in the gallery. Beuys wrapped himself in a felt mantle, which the coyote snatched at and worried from time to time, and he carried a herder's staff and a musical triangle.

Like Friedhelm Mennekes and other observers of Beuys' performances, New York author David Levi Strauss believed that the artist's
shows were pregnantly symbolic rituals. See Strauss' encyclopaedic
consideration of I like America and America Likes me in between dog
& wolf: Essays on Art and Politics (Brooklyn: Autonomedia, 1999).

"Mythologically and biologically," we read there, "Coyote is a survivor and exemplar of evolutionary change. This is what attracted
Beuys to Coyote. Beuys embraced the coyote as a progeny of the paleo-
Siberian, Eurasian steppe-wolf that came across the Bering Strait
12,000 (or more — some estimates go as high as 50,000) years ago and
adapted to its New World home. Coyote carried the paleo-Asiatic shamanic knowledge with him, spread it through the North American
West and in Mesoamerica." The animal known to zoologists since 1823
as Canis latrans "symbolized the wild and untamed, an unacceptable
threat to husbandry, domesticity, and law & order." A campaign of
extermination has been waged against the American coyote for the
last 200 years, without success; the animal flourishes on prairies,
pastures, in urban parks and ravines, in woodlands adjoining cities.
In the mythology of Beuys, the coyote is the ineradicable id, the political and cultural underground of our secular, mass-democratic North
American cities that is both a threat, and our last hope.

Medical imagery abounds in Beuys' work. His "intentions in the
Coyote action were primarily therapeutic," Strauss writes. "Using
shamanic techniques appropriate to the coyote, his own characteristic
tools, and a widely syncretic symbolic language, [Beuys] engaged the
coyote in a dialogue to get to 'the psychological trauma point of the
United States' energy constellation'; namely, the schism between native intelligence and European mechanistic, materialistic, and positivistic values." On this accounting, the modern West was sick, sick of
itself, in need of medical treatment, nigh on death, a candidate for the
spa, where we could at least rest after the exhausting labour of con-
structing the West.

Certain Westerners were saying this at the start of the twentieth
century. Joseph Beuys believed it in the last third of that century. Then
everyone did. In the early years of the twenty-first century, millions

in the cities of Europe and North America believed the modern West was finished. Islamic militants in western Asia believed it. Vast numbers in Russia believed it. Dreams of the reportedly glorious Muslim caliphate revived. Dreams of a Eurasian empire dominated by Russia were rekindled. What Beuys was said by Strauss to have believed, when he sheltered with a coyote for three days in 1974, had become the doctrine of the age only a few decades later.

Strauss: "Among the Ohlone peoples who once lived in what is now the San Francisco Bay Area, vision seekers going out (in dream) to contact animal-helpers had to be very careful. These animal-gods [according to Malcolm Margolin, in The Ohlone Way, *San Francisco: Heyday Books, 1978] were 'amoral, unpredictable, greedy, irritable, tricky and very magical. Cultivating such helpers was a complicated, exasperating and often dangerous undertaking'."*

⤳ 29

The summer my father was murdered, my mother's gardener stopped trimming the green lawn that surrounded the white house at Spring Ridge. Tall weeds sprang up before the near-tropical Southern summer was over, and, one afternoon in August, Essie discovered a snake in the weeds and killed it with a shovel. Other animals found their ways from the forest, across the cotton fields and into the yard and into my mother's rose garden, and I was not afraid of any of them.

One was a coyote, and it killed and ate my cat. Having killed once, it came back another time in August, and would have eaten something else, had Essie not shot it with one of my father's rifles. It did not die right away. It lurched and stumbled around in a wide circle for a while, trying to hide itself. After the coyote died among the weeds on the green lawn, black-winged buzzards with naked heads flapped down from the sky, and they pecked and clawed the carcass until I came running through the tall weeds that had grown up on the derelict lawn and chased them off, again and again.

Had Essie not shot the coyote that later died, had I known then what I know now, I could have snared it and brought it into a room in the white house and lived with it there for three days. It would have torn at the blanket I wrapped myself in, since coyotes, I have been told, dislike secrets. It would have worried the crooked, blind-man's cane my father brought me from Mexico, where he went each year to hunt deer and mountain sheep, and that now, since his death, I carried with me everywhere like an ensign, because he had given it to me. The house would no longer have been something white and entire, something standing white and complete on the green lawn, had the coyote dwelt with me there for three days. The house would have become contaminated by a scent that was neither wild nor tame, the odour of neither wolf nor dog, because coyotes belong to the borderline. Then I, too, could have been impure.

Years before I arrived, when its photograph was taken for the billboard by the river, the Occidental Hotel had been white and pure, and no coyotes trespassed the long boundary Mr. Steinway defended with poisons and traps. There had been an ideal balance of terror, as there was in the great world beyond the hotel, and all was at peace. That was the era Mr. Steinway remembered most fondly of all. In those days, the hotel was filled every summer by holiday-makers from the city, by young people, the men among them veterans of the mid-century conflict, all of them materialists. Their little children had white, straight teeth. It was during those summers that friendly deer came up to the parking lot out of the forest gloom, seeking the peanuts that guests often brought them, thrusting their muzzles into the outstretched hands of teenagers half-frightened because they had never before been so close to wilderness.

Mr. Steinway remembered with pleasure those summers in the epoch of mutually assured destruction, and he spoke about them for hours into the voice recorder of a serious young woman who was writing a book about the decline and fall of the mountain resorts. He talked at unusual length of the famous people he had welcomed as guests, such as Henry Kissinger, Lucille Ball, I.B. Singer, and the popular novelist Janet M., who was known to her fans as Rudolph Sandman.

One evening, while I was heaping logs on the grate of the immense lobby fireplace, Mr. Steinway told me that he personally knew Rudolph Sandman, who died of a brain haemorrhage in the Occidental's yoga studio when demonstrating the "downward dog" position for other female guests. Janet M. told the weeklies that she always wrote her best fiction after a round of spa treatments at the Occidental, which, she said, inspired her. Be that as it may, her novels were set in hotels that could hardly have been less like this one — not sprawling and new and democratic like the Occidental, but rather petite (yet grand in attitude, and very European), and her fictional hotels were peopled with penniless counts stealing into the bedrooms of neurotic debutantes, anxious young men plotting spectacular suicides, plutocrats betraying their home-bound wives, and other characters of a degraded sort.

The summer crowd at the Occidental during the years around the Cuban missile crisis, in contrast, was composed of honest, tedious sons and daughters of toil, as Mr. Steinway called them. They were entrepreneurs and middle-men and housewives who lived in the city's post-war suburbs, whose parents had been Communists in the city's garment district long ago, and immigrants before that — but they, the parents, were now warehoused in homes for incurables. When at home, the guests lived with several modern appliances and, unlike their teenaged children, were thrifty and clean, tidy and fond of martinis. At least, that is what Mr. Steinway said they were. I never met one of them, since they had all stopped coming to the Occidental before I arrived, or perhaps they were all dead by that time.

Had I lived with the coyote in the white house for three days, I would have learned about something that was not wild and that was not tame, something that was neither the Blue Hole nor the white house of my father, and I would have acquired its scent. The smell would have set the hands of men and women against me, as they are against the coyote, but this scorn would have kept me sane. It would have kept me from hankering for the peace of the Blue Hole or, later, the purity and quiet of the Occidental Hotel — frictionless places, where all dissonance ceases, or where I imagined this to be the case. I watched the coyote bitch from my window in the room with aqua plastic wall-covering while she tugged and gnawed the stag's guts at the edge of the parking lot.

30

Alexander, the important child, did not leave the Occidental Hotel when the other travelling folk checked out. He watched the coyote with me, and saw her, as I did, becoming sated and lazy and careless, dozing in the sunny, shadowless parking lot for hours with her muzzle tucked under her front paws. Alexander wanted to shoot her with Mr. Steinway's rifle, a deed that would have pleased Mr. Steinway considerably, but I said, no, I ran off the buzzards when Essie killed the coyote at Spring Ridge, and there was to be no killing of this one.

So Alexander and I stalked this one where she lay, lazy and careless, and half-tame by the looks of it, near the carcass of the stag. She stood up, then trotted away a short distance, when we approached her with the tackle and gear of capture. But then she became curious, and came back closer, finally sniffing our equipment.

We lived with her for three days in a white room in the Occidental Hotel, asking her questions she could not answer, making up answers to fill the silence. She urinated on copies of the *Wall Street Journal* that we spread on the floor, and soon the room was filled with a scent that was not wild and that was not tame.

We asked her what is it like, being something that is not wild and that is not tame, and we invented this answer: that it is like being shut up in a white room with a coyote, it is like being wrapped in a blanket that holds in the injured body's heat, and having the coyote snatch at it, tear it away in fits and starts. My injury occurred when the body of my father slipped away from me and sank without me into the depths of the Blue Hole. I could have followed the coyote I saw on the river bank then and there, not waiting, and become impure. Instead, I saw the billboard that advertised the Occidental Hotel, which was clean and white, and I wanted it and followed the traces of it until, after many years, the time came for me to approach the front desk.

We asked her, this survivor of poisons and traps, what it is like, living with us in the Occidental Hotel, and we devised this answer: that it is like being odd in a city of the West during the first decade of the Cold War, when the hotel's guests allegedly shared certain verities and pieties that made their transit across years seem easy, or at least predictable. Then, there were easily identifiable herders, with herders' crooked staffs, to guide the flock and make plain their ways before them — or so I remembered from my childhood in the South. Thereafter, the shepherds went away, or died off, or merely became unbelievable, and careers became unpredictable, if they existed at all any longer.

We asked her what she was. Because she did not know, or because she could not tell us, we made up an answer. The coyote, I said, was a story composed of all the stories told about coyotes by men and women and recorded by them since the beginning of history — tales of tricksters, shamans, travellers between worlds, cunning ones, ones who carried their vulvas in boxes on their backs. She was the sum of these projections, I said to her, yet I knew in my heart that she was none of them, certainly not the sum of them. She was only a small American mammal in a white room at the Occidental Hotel, and, in an important sense, the story ends there, with that dense fact. My father was a dead mammal I let go, even as I let the living coyote go at the end of three days, being unable to bear any longer the distance that yawned between us and her.

Indeed, for the time Alexander and I lived with the coyote bitch we had captured at the edge of the parking lot, the boundary between us and her, our world and her world, was firm, unsmudged by sentimentality. Nothing made the fixity of this divide more clear than the different reeks of our urine and her urine on the floor, on the newspapers spread there, and her persistent snatching at the mantles we wrapped ourselves within. No communion occurred between us and her, contrary to the expectations of the age's late romanticism.

But something impure was made inside the Occidental Hotel, something that was not wild and that was not tame, that was not like the hotel, comfortable and abstract, and I am telling you this because it happened to the coyote and to Alexander and me. Had he known about it, Mr. Steinway would have called the thing unnatural, because it did not come into existence in accordance with the law of the hotel, the rational, efficient law of the epoch in which the Occidental Hotel was built, and that was what he knew. Here was a new law—improbable, unheard of, governing ephemeral occurrences—and we lived under it for just three days, which was long enough to create something unnatural and beautiful, that countermanded the law of the Occidental Hotel, if only for three days. It could not have gone on for more days than that, since the nature of its law was to be fleeting, of a moment, then gone.

∼31

The noise within the white room we shared with the coyote was the whining whirr of turbines powered by oil. It came from deep inside the Occidental Hotel, from the place that generated the electricity coursing through the hotel's enormous network of wires. Mr. Steinway had once held all the keys and codes to the place of the turbines strictly in his personal keeping, but he long ago turned them over to a small bureaucracy of managers recruited from towns in the vicinity. After the travelling folk checked out and the hotel closed that autumn, leaving Alexander and me the only guests, the small bureaucracy dispersed, taking the keys and codes with them, allowing the turbines to spin on and on automatically.

In the summer that Essie shot the coyote on the green lawn, my father took me to the cotton gin. I watched and listened to the oily black steel machinery, which, deafeningly clanking and rattling, tore the seeds from the fibres, then pushed the cleaned white cotton into the hydraulic press that crushed it into tight bales. A cloud of lint was made molten and glowing by long shafts of sunlight admitted by perforations in the corrugated metal skin of the building. The lint-thick air smelled of hot weather, sweat, machine oil and cotton, smells that were also the odours of my father and of the South he came from. I never again smelled him, living or dead, after that afternoon in the cotton gin, since he went away to meet his murderers the same day, and my mother buried his body somewhere I could not find it before she told me he was dead.

The turbines deep inside the Occidental Hotel spun throughout the days Alexander and I lived with the coyote bitch, asking her questions she could not answer. Mr. Steinway did not know she was inside the hotel. Had he known, he surely would have objected, even though the owner had abandoned him, if only because of the stench of our urine and hers, which filled the white room. Like the smells of the cotton gin, which were old, very old, the sounds in the white room were old, very old, rolling up from a time before this one, a time, even, before that of the new home of the Occidental Hotel, whose time and whose law was white and pure and clean.

Like the smells in the room, and the smells of my father, the whine of the turbines we heard belonged to a time before that of the hotel, even though the machines were in the hotel somewhere. We did not know exactly where, but the emplacement must have been in what Mr. Steinway called "the old part," the remaining fragment of the building from the early twentieth century that had been otherwise demolished at the beginning of the Cold War, when the modernist Occidental that I knew was constructed all around it.

The guest rooms and the turbines were situated far apart in that reconstruction, to insure that the machinery would not disturb anyone, that no-one would even know it existed. But Alexander and I could clearly hear the machines turning in a place very near the white room.

Eli Whitney's invention of the mechanical gin has been praised for the surge in the South's cotton-based economy during the early nineteenth century, and blamed for the consolidation of negro slavery as the key pillar upholding Southern white society, thus for the onset of the Civil War. There was no negro slavery in the South my father came from — no, there was another law, the law we lived by, the one I learned when my mother punished me for swimming naked with Essie's negro son in Mr. Sam Hall's pond, the one I learned when I visited the cotton gin and black faces backed away from my father into the shadows as he spoke angrily. The pounding rattle of the gin, clawing seeds from the white fibre, was very loud, and they were the sounds of a world that existed before my father died and the Cold War began, and before I left Spring Ridge.

The whine of the turbines in the heart of the Occidental Hotel filled the air of the white room in which Alexander and I lived with the coyote bitch for three days. Had they been able to hear it, the sound would have appalled the guests who summered there during the Cold War, since it vividly recalled the mechanical din of the garment sweatshops their parents had worked in before growing old and ill and moving into homes for incurables. But they could not hear it, and nothing else reminded them of pasts they had left behind. The sounds they heard were the clink of champagne glasses raised in celebration of the lives the Cold War had given them, the clatter of dishes being gathered up in the Tamarack Dining Room, the dance music of orchestras Mr. Steinway booked in the city after the owner ceased to appear.

According to Mr. Steinway, the owner, an American, bought the old hotel building during the Second World War, knocked down all of it except the part where the turbines were housed, then put up the new concrete and white-clad resort in harmony with the law of the new era. It was an immediate sensation. Couples, often accompanied by small children, drove into the mountains from the city's suburbs, left their cars in the vast parking lot, checked into spacious rooms stacked like cells in a beehive, stayed for weeks.

The owner maintained an interest in, even a kind of curiosity about, the place throughout the early Cold War. He had it photographed, and he sold picture postcards of it for 25 cents per item. He had the image on the postcard blown up to billboard size, and mounted on the sign in the city through which ran the river I sat by at midnight, thinking of drowning. From this image, nobody could have guessed there were turbines inside, grinding out electricity. From the look of it, the Occidental Hotel was a pure, complete block, so much brightness frozen into a spare geometrical certainty silhouetted against the china-blue sky.

Figure 5: A photograph taken during the action entitled *Iphigenia/Titus Andronicus*, which the German artist Joseph Beuys staged, on 29 and 30 May 1969, for experimenta 3, an avant-garde theatre festival in Frankfurt-am-Main. The artist appeared on the flood-lit stage clad in a long fur coat (which he took off almost at once) and his usual felt fedora and canvas fisherman's vest. A white horse stood, grazing on hay, upstage from Beuys. The horse stood on a metal plate that served as an audio pick-up device, capturing and amplifying the otherwise inaudible sounds of the horse's hoof-movements.

According to Philippe Bettinelli, who may have been present for the performance, Beuys soon discarded the coat and started making "guttural sounds" into a microphone, biting off mouthfuls of fat and then spitting them out, crashing together two large bronze cymbals, mimicking birds. Other sound was provided by the playing of tape-recorded excerpts from Shakespeare's bloody revenge play Titus Andronicus *and Goethe's verse drama* Iphigenie auf Tauris. *Another report of the performance claims that Beuys himself muttered lines from Goethe's play. I am inclined to believe he did not do so.*

Beuys maintained throughout his career that, when, in 1944, the Stuka dive-bomber he was flying in crashed on Crimean soil, Tatars found his almost lifeless body in the wreckage, wrapped him in fat and felt, and thereby revived him. Several critics have shown this story to be fiction. Bettinelli, as translated by Anna Knight, wrote that "by associating himself with an animal, through the fur and the bird imitations, [Beuys] evokes the transformations of Tartar Shamanic rites, such as the substitution of Iphigenia in extremis by a deer on the pyre that was destined for her. The action is therefore intended to represent an overall renaissance, through the acceptance of a positive and lost form of animality."

The ancient Greeks knew Crimea as Tauris.

Instead of "accepting" animality, as Bettinelli asserts, Beuys was rejecting society, or the proposition that something defined as society or culture might exist. Oblivion, viz. nature, exists; nothing else.

~**32**

In the weeks that followed the interview in the classroom, Jupp and his teacher tramped together on several Sundays through the spring and early summer countryside. Neither attended services in any church: Herr Fröhlingsdorf, because he was militantly anti-Christian, though no worshipper of the old northern gods whose cults certain Party functionaries had sought to resurrect; Jupp, because he found Kleve's Catholicism bookish and antique and incomprehensible, devoid of the excitement that the Hitler Youth gave him, too much of a piece with his parents' unfelt, routinized piety. Later, after the war, Jupp will find another hero in Wagner's Parsifal, the foolish youth made compassionate by witnessing the agony of the wounded Fisher-King, and heterodox, gnostic seeds, fallen on the ground of his mind, as we shall see, in the nineteen-thirties, will sprout and flourish and flower—but not then, in early 1937, when he was still fascinated by his flair for drawing, and by what he found to draw.

Jupp sketched spring blooms, or he nipped them off, then inserted them into the belted flower press he carried slung over his shoulder. He learned from his teacher, if he did not already know, what wild plants lived and thrived in the beech stands and on the margins of meadows where livestock grazed, and what his teacher called degenerate life-forms, failures on the last, losing stretch of their evolutionary struggle.

Not long after they began to take these hikes, Jupp decided the time had come to share secrets. He guided his companion to the secluded glade in which he thought he had spotted a hunting wildcat, a great rarity. He took him to the cattle pond where the frogs sang loudest. He showed him the habitat, beside a small, slow stream, of a bright green moss, a loamy pelt of which they dug up to take home for study under the microscope. Beside the wide Rhine, or in low-lying meadows, or on the edge of rape fields, they lunched on the asparagus and loaves of *Bauernbrot* and wurst packed for them by the teacher's wife, Ingvild, and — guardedly at first, because of the chasm that separated German teacher and student in that era, but soon with more ease — they talked.

In boyhood and youth, Herr Fröhlingsdorf told Jupp, he explored the Hessian hills and the valley of the Lahn near his native town of Marburg, and, with his father, a philologist attached to the University of Marburg, reverently visited the Hessian and Westphalian hamlets and farms in which, it is said, the Grimm brothers first heard their fairy tales. He became interested very early by nature, especially the green things, and felt joy in knowing the names and virtues and secret bodily workings of plants. He was told by his father that boys who knew this joy could become men called botanists and know it forever. So, upon passing his *Abitur* in the relatively tranquil middle period of the Weimar Republic, he applied for, and was granted, admission to the University of Marburg's natural sciences faculty.

Coming, as he did, from an academic family, Michael Fröhlingsdorf was expected to be a serious student. Michael's father was the model for such seriousness. After imperial Germany crushed the 1904–1907 native risings in its African possession of Namibia, his father did important linguistic field-work among Herero-speaking women and children in the colony's Shark Island detention camp. The research at the prison, the elder Fröhlingsdorf claimed in a 1912 lecture to fellow scientists in Berlin, had advanced the understanding of Herero dialects, though it would have been more fruitful had his intelligent young informants not kept dying. Until the day of his own death, in 1941, he believed that the wresting of Namibia and the other colonial holdings from Germany at Versailles was infamous, wrong, and he laboured unwearyingly over his life's principal project, the critical modernization of the nineteenth-century Herero grammar and dictionary written by his intellectual hero, the German missionary Carl Hugo Hahn. Michael did not tell Jupp that Hahn's efforts, like those of many other productive scholars, were sustained by a devoted servant and comforter, Urieta (Johanna Maria Gertze). Michael's father always regretted his failure to bring home from Namibia a literate, Herero-speaking companion like Hahn's Urieta — a woman who could be, at once, mistress and secretary and research tool. Michael's mother spoke only German and French, the latter badly, but she did not prevent her husband's ascent to eminence in the late German empire's hive of scholars.

Michael, son of this distinguished father, dutifully fulfilled his family's expectations, was indeed an assiduous student of science, for a while. Then, he told Jupp, the dryness, narrow focus, and the stale professionalism of the biology lectures and demonstrations began to frustrate him. He recalled a particularly galling presentation, on the cytology of amoebas, that was so tedious and positivistic, so detached from any matter in life he considered urgent, it made him think of abandoning his science course and taking up literature. He knew he had a good mind for facts, but empirical facts in themselves were useless, like ships scuttled on the edge of an ocean they had been designed and built to traverse, to plumb, to open. He did not yet have a politics, but he wanted, in his studies, the soul of nature that had moved him when he walked, as a boy, through the countryside of Hesse.

Around the time he had his unfortunate encounter with amoebas, he continued, he made the acquaintance of other science students who shared his disaffection with the biology lecturers. Over Pils and pigs' knuckles in Marburg's Bückingsgarten on their first night out together, Herr Fröhlingsdorf and his new friends complained long about the sterile, mechanistic affair that modern science had been turned into. It had become, they agreed, technique and materialistic fact-mongering and empty experimentalism lacking all sense of the organic wholeness of life, any appreciation of the instinct to overcome that gives nature's wholeness its dynamic.

And who has done this? rhetorically asked a girl from Kiel named, teutonically, Ingvild. She was the daughter (Herr Fröhlingsdorf later learned) of a naval officer killed while on submarine duty in 1916.

The Jews who control everything in this rotten republic, that's who, grumbled a zoology student surnamed Morbach. There were noddings and assenting grunts on both sides of the beer-hall table. Ingvild Brauck then spoke up, hesitantly at first, but movingly, from her heart, for the beleaguered Nazis. They were the only political force in Germany, she said, that could end the corruption, the depravity of culture and science inspired by the Jews and leftists who ruled Germany, the only political faction that knew Germany's Jewish-Bolshevist enemy for what he was. Any German with scientific imagination, she said, should support the Nazis, since they were on the side of life against death, the nation's health against the viral sickness being spread by Jews and democrats and sexual deviants in high places.

She was wrong about Jews in Weimar Germany, of course. They were decadent only to the degree most Germans of the period were, certainly not more so. All they had ever wanted, since their emancipation from the ghetto in the nineteenth century, was to assimilate, to disappear into the German population, become mere Germans. By 1920, they had largely succeeded in turning themselves into respectable Germans, whatever the hysterically anti-Semitic press might have been saying to the contrary. The danger, in any case, was vastly exaggerated, as it always is in anti-Semitic thought, which I abhor. Jewish women dressed like German women, prepared German meals for their husbands and children. Jewish men all over Germany had their foreskins surgically restored, and their sexual practices were identical to those of Germans. Jews never aspired to be anything other than Germans, even after Germans started to tell them they could not be. They were not permitted to become Germans in Germany, so they went elsewhere and became Germans there. Today, they have a state of their own, one quite like the Germany whose racial policies they survived — nationalistic and militant, united and mobilized by healthy fear of what is alien to the dominant race, self-admiring and proud and determined to be invincible, hungry for respect, but virile enough to demand respect on its own terms, not those of others. It is an honourable state, as the South sought to be until its military defeat and Americanization — as the South could be again, if it followed the example of the Jewish racial state, and rediscovered sanity.

⌒ 33

This was the first time, in 1926, that I had ever met Nazis, keen ones anyway, Herr Fröhlingsdorf recalled one Sunday, as he and Jupp lunched under an oak not far from the Rhine. And this was also the moment that I began to wake up politically — something you Hitler Youth don't wait to do until you are at the old age of 19. But this was during the time of the Weimar system, and there was a lot of confusion that has been put to rest now. Germany walks in the sunshine today, science has found its soul again, he said, gathering his lean, tall frame off the ground beneath the tree.

And that young woman in the beer hall is now Frau Fröhlingsdorf? Jupp asked, who had heard from his mother that the couple met in university and suddenly — too suddenly, according to the gossip in Kleve — eloped and married. He stood up and began to assemble his sketchbooks and other paraphernalia.

You're right, the teacher said laughing, she is. I suppose there are no secrets in a little place like Kleve.

But Michael Fröhlingsdorf did, of course, have secrets.

He did not tell Jupp that, while still in high school, he had heard from the elder Fröhlingsdorf (who disapproved, being conservative, Protestant, nationalist, anti-French, but not a fervent anti-Semite) about students at the university who were turning to the Nazis. The scholar of the Herero language despised Nazis as upstarts, a bad, noisy lot, and, before his son Michael began his classes, he warned him to stay clear of them.

Everyone Michael had grown up among during the crisis-enfeebled early years of the Weimar Republic talked endlessly about politics, at meals, in the drawing room to which the family retired after dinner, taking with them the guests with whom they had dined, who themselves talked on and on — but the boy was interested in none of it, preferring to spend his free hours alone in the woods or alone in his room, reading popular scientific magazines. Because he had never imagined being anything else, he was a conservative of a certain unthought, old-fashioned sort. His parents were of this kind, and, having a compliant nature at this stage in his life, he had never rebelled against his upbringing among Bismarckian furnishings, tastes and ideas. Hence the little flinch, the slight, momentary resistance of his body, which he told Jupp nothing about, upon hearing Ingvild Brauck and his other complaining class-mates attack the Jew, a target of scorn off-limits in the home of the professor, who, as a boy, had been presented to Bismarck.

But Michael's hesitation and faint unease evaporated as Ingvild continued to speak. He heard her say that the sick, squabbling regime that so oppressed the German spirit deserved contempt, and no support from the young, or from anyone whose blood ran hot in his veins. The time had come for young people to forge a new German science that did not, like bourgeois Western science, confine itself to digging up and hoarding dusty nuggets of empirical fact and passing them on mechanically, but that would join the struggle for what is healthy, straight, destined to triumph, and against all which is doomed to perish in the eternal struggle at the heart of history, both natural and human.

The basic intellectual and cultural architecture of her remarks was, of course, not new. Obsession with physical and spiritual health, inspired by worry among Germany's newly urbanized and industrialized millions about criminality, disease and malformed souls, had been seething in the nation's popular imagination for decades before Ingvild was born, in 1907. Adoration of classical beauty and purity, deep dread of contamination — serious values largely abandoned in the present-day South, and, indeed, throughout depraved Western culture — were adumbrated constantly in all German media and in the very shape of the German language, and, long before his adolescence, they had informed Michael's consciousness, his young mind's ways of knowing and framing experience and the world, apolitical though he surely was as a teenager.

In the attack by the United States on the Confederate league in 1861, in the descent into war forced upon Germany in 1939 by the cosmopolitan enemies of the national idea, history witnessed tragic assaults on the instinctually sound resistance to the materialism and rot and effeminacy that distress me now, in this moment, as I write these words in the Occidental Hotel, though thinking of my grandmother's house in the South, a house scented by atoms of her fine face powder suspended in the still, humid air, by the toilet water my grandmother splashes on her throat in the afternoon, when the air in her rooms upstairs is warm and close. I smell her body pass in the dim, wood-panelled corridor outside the library that opens, through French doors, onto the porch shadowed by wisteria blossoms dripping from brawny, twisting vines. My father and his friends danced on this porch under Japanese lanterns glowing dusky red and orange in the darkness of Hallowe'ens in the distant past, long before I was born, when my father was a youth, steady and strong as an oak.

Late one radiant summer evening when I was turning from a boy into a youth, after my father was murdered and my mother died and I had come to live in this house, my grandmother ordered a negro to hang up paper lanterns the colour and shape of tangerines on the porch and light the tiny candles in them, and she danced with me slowly in the twilight and into the night, just the two of us, as she had danced with my father at Hallowe'en years before. She said that I was strong and steady as an oak, like my father in his youth and young manhood. Then she said I could now remember him as he was on that Hallowe'en night long ago, since I had danced with her as he had, had *been* him, and now I could forget everything else I knew about him — the sensual, disturbing odour of his body after he had been in the hot cotton fields with the negroes all day, the rhythmic plunging of his body into the unknown woman in the motel on the frayed edge of a city in the South.

But I could not forget him, cannot now forget him, any more than Michael could (if he had wanted to, which he had not) stifle his arousal by Ingvild's raging against weakness and against political and social modernity. He did not tell Jupp, on the Sunday he and the boy lunched not far from Rhine, that he despised, with vehemence he had not felt before, the things she despised, merely because she despised them. Michael did not tell Jupp that he watched, across the beer-hall table harshly lit by swags of incandescent bulbs, Ingvild's body breathing, moving slightly to the music of her violent sentences beneath the pale grey blouse with mother-of-pearl buttons, beneath the skirt the colour of dusty roses, beneath the thin membranes that concealed from his eyes the flesh he wanted to possess.

~34

Remember, because Jupp cannot, the light suppers in Michael Fröhlingsdorf's flat after hikes in the spring of 1937, suppers prepared by Ingvild Fröhlingsdorf on the Sundays before Jupp knew she hated him. Remember the talks Jupp and his teacher carried on for hours, after supper, in Michael Fröhlingsdorf's library, which was furnished with a gluttonously fat leather club chair that swallowed Jupp's body whole, a carved colonial secretary with many drawers and compartments, some secret, a broad oaken work-table on which stood a large brass-barrelled microscope and lay a heap of journals and books in no order. The air in the brown room was scented by tanned hides, by gradually deteriorating paper and ink, by the fine dust of dried flowers — odours proper to an old gentleman's library, Jupp could have noticed, not one belonging to a man as young as Herr Fröhlingsdorf.

Jupp liked best, at first, the conversations that tacked close to the quotidian, that explicated the afternoon's unpacked haul of plants and observations, that assembled biological facts and bits of lore about it from the teacher's spacious knowledge and from the guides and textbooks and articles piled in the dark wooden cases of his workroom. The concrete facts cascading from Herr Fröhlingsdorf's mind and sources interested Jupp, but less than the man's voice that spoke them, which was deep, dark as coffee, resonant like the sound of cellos in the Wagner operas he had, as a solitary boy, raptly listened to.

At the times on Sunday evenings when they did not talk, Jupp and his teacher drew — Jupp still uncertainly, but with growing confidence in the powers he was discovering in himself; Herr Fröhlingsdorf with a stiff, mechanically exacting, transcribing hand — and the man commented on the boy's renderings, encouraged him to tighten up his still-sprawling line, admonished him, again, to avoid impressions and ellipses in his art.

And at times when they neither researched nor drew, Herr Fröhlingsdorf would speak, with gravity not entirely proper for his still-young years, on what he called the philosophical-racial idea, which Jupp liked to hear about, since the teacher's thoughts on the topic seemed to come from an address inside the teacher's mind very near its center. He told Jupp of the galvanic force of unsullied male friendship that pulsed in the Aryan racial soul, welding disparate men into the unconquerable unity that is the *Volk*. He spoke of the natural exclusivity of the tribe, about the cosmic consciousness, the sensuous apprehension of the world-soul, attained by the most highly evolved men, especially German ones, at the end of their valiant rise from individualism. He spoke about spirituality and soul and the ascent of species. Warming to his subject, Michael would tell Jupp, in these terms or others like them: We have come through an era in which rootless cosmopolitanism infected, nearly fatally, science and the arts, family life, everything of lasting value in our national culture. Sanity and health have triumphed in our homeland for the time being, though our purchase on the earth is tenuous. Germany is surrounded by enemies of life — Jews, Bolshevists, modernists, democrats, liberals — all sick with greed and envy, bent on the destruction of this precious thing, this inner Germany, that had taken root in European soil. It is up to you, the youth, he said, to be resolute — primitive even — in ways Germans have not been primordial since the migration of Germanic peoples from the Aryan homeland into the West. Our manhood, our science, are at stake. The world-historical struggle against the unnatural, unclean, in science and elsewhere, is your task, your destiny, as it is my own, within the limits of my talent.

Like the ideology of health and sickness the young Michael Fröhlingsdorf had absorbed from the German air he lived in, the points in the teacher's remarks were not new. Jupp had heard these sentiments expressed countless times over the years, at meetings of his Hitler Youth den, at school celebrations and in his racial hygiene class, in speeches by scientists and psychoanalysts and other authorities, in radio broadcasts, newsreels at the movie theatre, from loudspeakers in Kleve's Tiergarten. Though impatient at moments with the hectoring insistence of it, especially when he would rather play or shoot his rifle than listen to it, he believed the general drift of what was said, the paradigm and world view that shaped his own and the millions' apprehension of time and space. Everyone he knew in Kleve believed what the Party said about history and truth. The Jews in Kleve were reported to believe something else, fearful, unnameable.

What he felt upon hearing these words was no more novel than the words themselves. Jupp had been summoned to "world-historical struggle" countless times, each one touching off a thrill in his lower spine and loins to which he had been addicted since the onset of manhood. At sixteen, he was certainly old enough to have known men and women whom a speech by the Führer or Dr. Goebbels or some other high personage in the Party left in a kind of erotic frenzy in the head; and he had himself been ravished by sensuous political music more than once. Though he had not yet had sex with anyone, he knew lust very well, and he liked it in himself. He knew this quickening of longing, fantasies of conquest and of the obliteration of whatever resisted possession. Somewhere in the shadowy, dangerous suburbs of his consciousness, fears of menace to his young body's power luxuriated — dreads of contamination, defilement, the unnatural — because the presence of potentially crippling threats to his new-found masculine force made the pleasure of lusting so much more intense.

But Jupp listened with special, tantalized attention to the teacher, because this man was different from any other man he had known. He was not impressively muscular in the way official examples of German manhood were, but he was strong and tall, and Jupp wanted to be like him. Jupp loved him more each time they went into the field and talked in his study; and Jupp was sure Herr Fröhlingsdorf loved him in return

— so much, in fact, that the older man had declared his reliance on Jupp to defend civilization, even science, from their slanderers and enemies. Jupp was flattered by the teacher's appeal to him, aroused by it, as youths are in whom latent vanity, curiosity and self-importance have been suddenly shaken awake by the nearness of power.

Ingvild Fröhlingsdorf washed and rinsed the dishes after supper, then stacked the wet plates and cutlery in the metal drying rack beside the sink. Dwelling most of the time in a sunny room of her mind that had been decorated by theory, she imagined she ought to enjoy washing and rinsing and stacking the dishes after she fed one or more of Michael's students, who frequently stopped by the flat for help with assignments, for more general counsel or because they were in love with him — the several questing students who then, at Michael's invitation, always stayed to eat. After the first couple of Sundays, Jupp did not wait to be invited to eat. It had come to be assumed by all, Ingvild noted, that supper would be ready soon after he and Michael returned from their walks in the country. Nothing further needed to be said.

Michael was generous that way, generous, that is, with Ingvild's time and patience. Early in their marriage, she had admired his hospitality, his kindness even to the slow pupils he taught. But the time had come for him to change. He was about fifteen years older than his students — too old to be the helpful, encouraging big brother he sometimes acted like, in her view. He should be fatherly, demanding, stern with the students. As it was, he was something between a big brother and a father, so the pupils, whom she resented, lazily exploited him, and encouraged what she took to be his own lazy streak. She wouldn't mind feeding them were they university students, future scientists, scholars in training, young men and women who gave Michael intellectual excitement, who challenged him with their questions. That would be different, and it would be different were she a professor's wife, with a servant to cook and clean up.

When she married Michael, quickly, after a liaison that sometimes seemed on the brink of turning passionate, she thought he might some-day find a post in a biological research institute or a university. He was good at his studies, but, as things turned out, not good enough. So Michael joined the civil service, and they came to Kleve, where Michael liked teaching high school biology and racial science, where he got on with his writing about race for the Party's publishers in Munich, where he lived in what seemed to be, after the squalor and dislocation of the Great Depression and the violent years on both sides of the Nazi acces-sion to power, a becalmed moment in Germany's twentieth century, which had been distracting and violently abstract between 1914 and 1933. There were jobs for all who were not Jewish or work-shy, good things in the bakeries and butchers' shops, abundances of movies, radios, detergents, parades, all outpouring generously from the state and the corporations into the hands of the people. There was no war, though thoughts and gestures and couplings were being increasingly militar-ized, which Michael thought appropriate in a nation hedged about by enemies of the idea, still menaced within by subtle poisoners, reaction-aries. The streets and squares were free of unrest. The Jews who had not migrated abroad seemed less threatening. Resisting them openly had become less urgent, especially since the summer of the Olympic games. Having made no compromises with conscience or sacrifices of conflicted will to obtain peace, Michael, in Germany during the spring of 1937, had peace.

Alexander must know that Ingvild did not. While she enjoyed a measure of prestige among the wives of Kleve's shopkeepers, artisans, policemen, doctors and dentists, she loathed the small-change gossip the other young women traded, their endless fussing over children, their unhastening, repetitive chat about prices in the shops along Adolf-Hitler-Strasse, and about how good things were for Germans these days. She believed things were good, though she did not want to be told

so again and again by women she did not like. She believed in the goodness of this frictionless condition, which she knew was maintained in
the only way it ever can be, by force and the subjection of the forced.
She had wished for this condition, she told Michael shortly after they
met, since the morning in November, 1918, when her brother Willi
died. That, she said, was the day she awakened.

The flat in Kiel that she inhabited with Willi and her mother, and
her Aunt Marthe, whose apartment it was, where Ingvild had lived since
her father drowned with his submarine crew off the Adriatic island of
Pelagosa, agreeably overlooked the street, instead of facing a sooty brick
wall or opening down the maw of an airshaft. The mutinous, revolutionary German sailors, led by Bolsheviks, had occupied the train station that November day in 1918, and been joined there by soldiers who
brought more arms. Other soldiers and civilians, loyal to the Kaiser,
gathered their strength and waited for the moment to attack the rebels.

The street below the aunt's window was quiet and empty in the
early morning of the occupation. A few minutes before lunchtime, the
women, girl and boy heard shouts and gunfire in the street, the tattoo
of machine-gun bullets spattering the walls of apartment blocks that
crowded the sidewalk. Come away from the window, her mother shouted
at Willi, who watched young men dart from doorway to doorway, dodge
around corners, firing pistols and rifles at each other. It's a revolution,
I can see everything, he said, just before the bullet shattered the glass,
penetrated his face below the right eye, burst from the rear of his head,
scattering brains and blood on Aunt Marthe's idyllic landscape paint-
ings before burying itself in the plastered wall, near the ceiling, when
Ingvild's mother screamed.

Michael told Ingvild that the shot could have come from any of the
combatants in the street below the window, the revolutionaries or the
militiamen loyal to the Kaiser. As if she knew certainly or could have
known anything about the streets on that November morning in Kiel,
she said a hardened Bolshevik did it, who was bent on murder that
morning, who bolted into a doorway across the street to escape the
bullets, who glanced up and saw a little boy's curious face framed by a
window above the sidewalk, and decided to extinguish that innocence.

Early one Sunday in 1937, while packing his gear and lunch for the day's trek into the countryside around Kleve with Jupp, Michael said to Ingvild: You would be happier if you didn't think so much about the Party's leading woman.

I think about her hardly at all, Ingvild said.

You do, often, Michael said, I know you do, because you talk about what she says, what she does, how she dresses. Not everyone is cut out to rise high in the Party, or anywhere close to a place as high as hers. Anyway, I don't understand why you want to move up in the women's wing of the movement at all. If you want to be useful, double the hours you devote to collecting for Winter Aid. Get involved with the League of German Maidens, they're always looking for someone. There's nothing for a woman in politics; you know that.

Kleve is so small, she thought, but did not say. Then she said aloud: I thought —

You thought, Michael interrupted. You thought. If you were nursing a baby, you wouldn't have time to think. Think about that for a change.

He left. Ingvild thought about her womb, which did not conceive, even though, every Friday night, Michael's seed spurted into it. She thought about the women whom, she knew, mentioned her barrenness when she was out of earshot, and she thought that, except for her barrenness, she was more qualified than anyone she knew to champion, as

Frau Scholtz-Klink did so eloquently in talks around the country, the natural superiority of the male sex in the family and society, the bravery of a proper woman's single-minded devotion to home-making, the nobility of woman's selfless ministry to the needs of man, her partner and mentor in evolutionary and political struggle. Being radical, free of bourgeois prejudice, Ingvild believed these ideas about women and men — virtuous ideas held in contempt by the liberationists who manipulate public opinion under America's half-negro President — and she pondered unhappily the limits Michael put on her preaching and promotion of them. She thought, chafing, until the late afternoon hour when she had to start supper, since the return of Michael and Jupp was imminent. Then, while preparing supper, she thought about the dirty dishes she would clear and clean after supper, as the man and youth talked for hours or drew silently in Michael's study, while she, in the living room, browsed through newspapers and the scientific journals Michael subscribed to.

Ingvild opened the magazines, but the articles on science were too difficult for her — she had taken her biology studies at Marburg seriously until she quit to marry Michael and serve his ambitions and needs, though she was never as good at science as she would like to have appeared — or the articles were on subjects that did not interest her. She was more superficial than she admitted to herself, less in love with learning than with the image of herself as a woman who knew about science, could talk about it in intelligent society. Many women nowadays try to get above themselves, including women in the South, I have learned in the course of my research. Forsaking biological destiny, these women start down their ruinous path by desiring to attain what belongs only to man. Then they turn mannish, teach themselves to speak coarsely, take up sports at which only men should strive, prevent themselves, like whores, from conceiving, or they bear children certain to be perverse. I am not saying that Ingvild was as bad as the worst of these hard-faced women in the South, about whom my grandmother told me everything. Negro women, being closer to the wellsprings of nature, are usually not given to the vices common among white women these days, even Southern ones, especially them, traitors to their race.

After a while, Ingvild tired of acting curious about science, put away Michael's professional journals, then picked up an illustrated weekly, in which she came across the picture of a clean-shaven young white man with a thin-lipped, straight mouth, a strong jaw, and with serious, attentive eyes that gazed fixedly across a desktop stacked high with bird skins, and straight into the camera's lens. She thought he looked familiar, though the man he looked like was always photographed with a beard. Her eyes dropped to the cutline under the picture, and she was pleased to learn he was indeed the German she thought he was, an explorer and hunter, a celebrity of sorts since the publication, in 1933, of his successful real-life adventure book *Mountains, Buddhas and Bears,* which had thrilled her and many other Germans.

Exotic, densely action-packed, sometimes startling, always educational, and sprinkled with tales of calamities endured and overcome, the book narrates the German author's version of an often perilous, ostensibly scientific journey of discovery that took a small, American-led team, in 1931, upriver from Shanghai and the gaping mouth of China's Yangtze River, through territories violently contested by bandits, warlords, Communists, Nationalists and savage tribesmen, to a wild place on the eastern edge of the Tibetan plateau, from which the Yangtze descends to the cities of men. The author, whose appetite for the hunt was insatiable, compulsive since boyhood, became the second white man to shoot dead a giant panda in the wilderness. (The first to do so was an American. The hide of his victim is now at the Field Museum, in Chicago.) Driven by hunger for ornithological knowledge, his academic speciality, the author killed and skinned thousands of birds. He also killed many Chinese and Himalayan mammals, insects and spiders, the taxidermied remains of which, along with the bird hides, can be found today in Philadelphia's Academy of Natural Sciences, the sponsor of the adventure he took part in, and in German natural-history collections. He killed, as far as anyone knows, no men, other than, possibly, some marauders, probably Communists, whom he picked off with his Mauser when they attempted to raid the iron-clad boat on which he travelled upriver.

~**37**

When we hid among the steamer trunks, old hat boxes, dust-covered litter of broken furniture, stacks of books and magazines nobody had looked at in a hundred years, all in the attic of my grandmother's house one hot July afternoon, a visiting cousin, an adolescent male, whispered things to me about a mannish, coarse white woman in the Southern city near my grandmother's house, in the country, where I lived with Sister until I came to the Occidental Hotel. The white woman bore a grudge against the family and set out to ruin my father.

But the woman could not prove to the satisfaction of the judge, an acquaintance of my family, that my father had sired her daughter's infant son, and my father testified under oath that he had never carnally known the girl, though, my cousin whispered to me in the attic when I was 13, everyone in the family knew he did it. My cousin's mother, who was married to my grandmother's sister's son, had told my cousin that my father was always wild like that when he came home on leave from his military school in Virginia, and she told him my father probably acquired the girl on a street corner somewhere downtown, he was like that when he and Cousin Billy and some other boys who lived down in the country went riding around the city, drinking, after a Hallowe'en dance on the porch of my grandmother's house. The cousin said his mother had told him that my father would not leave the girl alone after that night with her, pestered her every

134

time he came home from school, kept at her until my grandmother stopped it.

I told my cousin he was a liar. He said his mother had told him the story, that everybody knew it was true. I told my cousin his mother was a liar. We fought in the suffocating attic, disturbing the dust of it, until my grandmother sent up her negro to pull us apart. After his father had taken the cousin home, my grandmother said both my cousin and his mother were liars, always had been, that side of the family was infested with liars. But I knew the story could have been true, since I had seen my father do it in a motel when I was a very little boy, before I had a name for it.

My elder brother, the son of my father's lover, a son whose existence was known only to me in the tale my cousin told me when I was 13, came looking for me on a winter morning after our grandmother died, when Sister was away, doing readings from her new book.

Since his childhood, the mother had nurtured in him the belief, for which there was no foundation in law or custom or promise, that money was due him after the death of my father, who had begotten and abandoned him. He said he had intended to leave me alone, he never wanted to cause any trouble, but his mother told him he was owed, so he thought about it a long time, and decided that she was right, that he was owed. He said my family's letting him grow up poor was wrong, with so much money and my grandfather's plantation in our hands, and — as my brother put the matter — with every judge and politician in the county screwed down and snapped down by us inside a Mason jar and stored in the pantry, like dewberries put up in the summer against the winter day one of us would want to eat them. He said he knew a secret about my father, more scandalous even than my father's repudiation of his son, and he would never tell it to a living soul if I gave him what he wanted.

He stood and talked at the edge of the hearth that, on the uncommon winter days when a norther blows through, warms the library in which I studied. My grandmother's negro had laid a small fire there a few minutes before my brother knocked at the kitchen door. My brother was middle-aged, and his troubles showed on him. His chest had slid downward and puddled inside a frayed, cheap white shirt that bellied out, like a canvas sail filled with wind, behind the tongue of his tie and over his belt buckle. The shabby suit he wore had not fit in years, unless the fleshy billowing of his body were new, which was possible. His tired eyes were brown, like tanned hide or sea-wrack, like mine. Soft as kid, and disagreeably flaccid, the right hand I shook when the negro showed him into the library, before I knew his business, told me he had toiled with his mind all his life, never with arms and back.

Though he had rehearsed many times what he would say to me in this moment, and though he had been urged on by his mother to lay before me a clear choice between paying or being shamed, he faltered, began to sweat when I told him to go ahead and do his worst. I had sensed correctly that he was an amateur at extortion, not a clever or adept blackmailer. When the time came for him to commit his sin, the thought of becoming a cowardly criminal perhaps caused some moral gristle deep inside his flabby body to twitch, unstarching his nerve. Or he realized he had no terrible secret, merely some tittle-tattle his mother had fed him and that everyone in the county already knew about. Or perhaps — this was most likely — he was, as his handshake and droopy physique indicated, a contemptible weakling, a disgrace to his sex and race.

He then sat down, without being invited to do so, and wept. From his snivelling, I gathered that he needed money because the divorce had bankrupted him, and because he wanted to get away from his ex-wife and his mother, from everything here. I asked him where he wanted to go. The mountains, he said. But not mountains in the South, like those in which the Occidental Hotel stands, nor ones anywhere in America, or even in Europe. Even the high ones in America and Europe, he said, are close to cities, where the rot is, everywhere the stench of people dying of cancer and radioactive contamination, where streets lined with skyscrapers clad in mirrored glass are haunted by dangerous mulattos quickened into existence by couplings of negro men and white women. Negro men leave the cities and go into the American mountains and find white women willing to couple with them, I know they do, he said, because I have seen negro men there, and this goes on even among the highest mountains of Europe. I want to go among mountains that are pure and clean, where clear melt-water from dazzlingly white glaciers plunges through steep, narrow valleys before slowing and emptying into the rivers that slake the thirst of the poisoned cities.

I rejected his escapism. I told him that the intellectual struggle for the inner South must be fought out here, on native ground. Flight is, or should be, unthinkable, however sordid or Americanized the South had recently become, or, indeed, *because* it had become sordid.

I read all the time, my brother said, especially now, when I'm out of work. I read books about mountains, all kinds of books about white explorers, but mainly old ones I find in the city library or in used-book shops — old books, because I tried to read a new one at some point, and didn't like it. In the old ones, white men successfully ford viciously turbulent rivers, press forward across wind-scoured, bleak tablelands, and eventually reach the highest, purest place on earth — where, one of the best old books says, the white race first learned its arts and secrets from hidden masters — a mysterious place guarded by Kangchengd-zonga, Xixiabangma, Gyachung Kang, all very high, very pure mountains. Even if they never climb to the summits — some things are beyond even the bravest human will — the men in the stories touch these shining mountains, having overcome procedural obstacles thrown in their paths by effeminate bureaucrats, mastered savage tribes warring in the foothills, faced down hunger and loneliness and lawlessness, and endured clouds of biting flies and suffocating dust, having conquered their disgust, natural for white men, with filthy lodgings in villages that stand knee-deep in excrement and the decaying carcasses of dogs and pack animals, having outwitted fanatical monks and thieving satraps, and shown themselves to be true men when tempted by conniving native women, armed with the allures of night, who menaced their manhood.

Like Don Quixote, I observed silently, my brother had been driven mad by reading stories of adventure. I asked him: You think you can stand firm when your manhood is thus menaced?

Of course, I gave him money, even more that he had asked for. I loved him then. He was going to Tibet, which Jupp had dreamed about in 1956, when he forgot to wash and would have forgotten to eat, had not his friend Nylons reminded him to do so.

The eyes of Ingvild, Michael's wife, dropped down below the picture, below the cutline under the picture, to the story.

So we find ourselves in the Berlin flat of the celebrated young scientist, hunter, author and SS Untersturmführer Ernst Schäfer, writes the English journalist Matthias Zimmermann in the weekly publication Ingvild reads in the living room, while Jupp and her husband talk in Michael's library.

The skin of an immense brown bear covers the floor of his study, the hides of birds are mounted on every square inch of wall not occupied by framed photographs or bookshelves stuffed with volumes and journals. Above the desk hangs a large 1931 picture of Herr Schäfer, neatly bearded, as he always is when on an expedition, smiling and vigorous, holding a dead bird by its head in one hand and, with the other, propping up the giant panda he has just brought down. Another picture, this one from 1935 — snapped surreptitiously, Herr Schäfer tells me, to avoid upsetting the sherpas, who are profoundly superstitious — captures the climactic moment in the ritual dismemberment of a high lama's corpse, just as the outcast who has been butchering the body pulls out the entrails and, with a loud shout, invites the waiting vultures to feast on the disjoined remains.

Of course, Herr Schäfer says, pointing to the photo of the so-called sky burial on his wall, the twentieth-century German mind is revolted by such barbarity, which, sad to say, has been endemic in Tibetan religious and intellectual culture since its rape and impregnation by Lamaism, a force entirely alien to the mental cast of Tibet's indigenous peoples. This colourful, intricate culture has keenly interested anthropologists and other European and American travellers for many years, but the further illumination of it will not be the primary mission of the German Tibet Expedition of 1938. Under my leadership, the team will study terrestrial magnetism, and collect specimens and seeds of the useful plants that have evolved in the harsh weathers of the Tibetan plateau — grains and legumes that might help Reich botanists breed hardier strains for European cultivation. We will test the theory, by careful measurement, that Tibet's native people had ancient intercourse with the Nordic racial type, and find and name species hitherto unknown to science. The aims are purely scientific. Our patron, Reichsführer-SS Himmler, himself a man interested in science, expects us to accomplish a great deal, to advance German science, and we plan not to disappoint him, or the German people.

You are famous, Zimmermann writes, for your books on the two American-led expeditions you accompanied to western China and Tibet, in 1931 and 1935. You are currently raising money for the 1938 effort, an exclusively German one. Will your renown in Germany be enough to attract the support of foreign museums and institutes?

I don't need their help, Herr Schäfer replies. We don't need the encouragement of cosmopolitan, presumably neutral institutions. In fact, I have had no trouble at all finding backers for the project in the Fatherland, proud Germans who understand the value of what we want to do. The Public Relations and Advertising Council of German Business has put up the greatest part of the budget, The *Völkischer Beobachter* has helped, and so has IG Farben. We still need some technical equipment, altimeters, theodolites and such, but I have no doubt it will be forthcoming. The manufacturer of the Olympia Plurotyp gave me a portable typewriter, wonderfully light, which I'll carry into Tibet and definitely make use of. I certainly don't expect to wait until I am back in Europe to get started on my memoir of our trip.

Zimmermann: The Council is a department in Dr. Goebbels' enlightenment and propaganda ministry and the *Beobachter* is the official

Party newspaper. Given your indebtedness to the state and the Party, can you guarantee that your research in Tibet will be disinterested, completely objective?

Schäfer: Of course it will be objective. I am, before all else, a zoologist with a focused interest and considerable experience in the field of ornithology. Each of my colleagues will be a specialist, a scholar, trained in the rigorous tradition of German science that stretches, unbroken, from the present back to Goethe and Alexander von Humboldt and Carl Friedrich Gauss. No relaxation of disciplinary standards will be tolerated on any venture I have anything to do with, and my colleagues are of one mind with me about this. We are not going to the roof of the world for a holiday, after all.

Each member of the Tibet team is, like you, a young SS officer. Why?

The answer should be self-evident. The officer corps is composed of the most intelligent, the most physically and morally fit and loyal men in Germany, so it was only natural for me to build up the team from the scientists among them, especially since the journey across the highest mountains in the world will be difficult, forbidding, even dangerous at times, which is the reason few scientists have attempted to make it. We SS officers are young, ready for anything, able to live as nomads if need be. I can imagine no school better than the SS to prepare men for travel on our hard road.

You will need considerable help when you're there.

Naturally. After crossing India and establishing camp in Sikkim — our last stop before entering Tibet, we will hire pack animals for the caravan, and we will recruit healthy young men like ourselves from the Himalayan kingdoms and tribes to haul instruments and gear, manage the mules and yaks, cook for us, clean and preserve and carry the specimens we collect. I have worked with boys of the sort we want on my expeditions with the Americans. Though exposed to bourgeois civilization by their British masters, many of them remain stalwart children of nature, uncorrupted, inured to the hardship we will face together. They will serve us well as bearers and guides and interpreters, and they will share all our adventures, which they will someday tell their grandsons about.

As an SS officer, you have sworn unquestioning obedience to the Führer. As a scientist, you are a hostage of empirical fact. You once said that you were completely free of conflict with regard to your various allegiances. Are you still?

Absolutely. What a question — but you are not really German, are you, despite your name? Only in America, or Britain, some country that knows nothing of our sort of national revolution, would it occur to any-one that to be both a man of science and a patriot is to invite twinges of conscience. The mission of the SS, to perfect nature, and the mission of true science are identical Both the SS man and the scientist strive to cut the way through superstition and reaction into the future, both seek to cleanse the world from error and impurity, both embody the spiritual and moral uprightness and unflinching insight into the human condi-tion typical of the Germanic racial type. Some of your questions make me suspect you belong to that crowd of bourgeois negativists — don't interrupt, you know very well they exist, even in today's Germany — who claim that my enthusiasm for National Socialist ideals makes it impos-sible for me to do unbiased research. They say that science must be an international enterprise. I do not disagree. The findings of research belong to all mankind. But the so-called internationalist individual, in the bourgeois-liberal sense, does not exist. Science, like art, always expresses the racial soul, the essence, the historic national imagination, of the man who does it. German science serves the *Volk*. We hide our motives from no-one. Tell that to the nay-sayers. The German Tibet Expedition will advance proudly under the banner of the SS and in the name of the *Volk*.

Won't that identification become problematic when you seek per-mission from the British to enter Tibet through the Himalayan passes they control?

That's another of your curious questions. Like all other Germans, and like most Britons, we want only peaceful relationships to subsist between the Reich and the United Kingdom, however different our national paths may be. My conscience is clear, I am a zoologist engaged in research, not a political agitator or spy, and I believe the colonial officials in London will appreciate the purity of my intentions. They surely have nothing to fear, in any case, from a tiny band of German scientists wanting to cross mighty India, exit, disappear into a little-understood country beyond the borders of their empire. If we need help persuading the bureaucrats, we can certainly call on the many eminent English friends of the new Germany. But I don't think that will be necessary. I anticipate no problems with London after we have been granted the right to enter Tibet by the government in Lhasa.

You have not secured their cooperation?

Not yet—these matters take time, we may have to be in India before the details are worked out—but, here again, I expect no difficulties. I understand the Regent, there being no Dalai Lama at the moment, is kindly disposed toward Europeans who come in peace and in a spirit of genuine curiosity. No, neither the Colonial Office nor the *Kashag* [the Tibetan government] is likely to oppose us. The great challenges we face are not political. They are the tests of our youth and fortitude posed by tremendous mountains, avalanches and storms and the lakes of mud we will have to cross, the thin air of the immense plateau beyond the highest peaks. We will have to overcome the resistance of simple people, addicted to the fabulous cosmologies and tall tales of Lamaism, to letting us measure and catalogue their skulls and skeletons. There will likely be some tut-tutting about our collecting of animals and birds they consider sacred, not to be killed, you know, even in the name of intellectual advancement. If the tales travellers have told are true, we will witness things even more repellent to German sensibility than the gruesome sky burial we documented, with its untouchable butchers and ravenous vultures. But, if we are fortunate and don't lose our nerve, we will also discover and photograph and film wonders of this secret world never before seen by European eyes.

Will you look for Shambhala?

No.

Many Germans would like to know if it exists, and where.

Yes, I am aware of that. The team will include experts in several fields, but folklore is not one of them. Now, your readers would probably be interested to learn more about what we *do* plan to accomplish. Tibet's carrion-scavenging birds, for instance, are known in the West—

—Your sponsor, the Reichsführer-SS. has created a scholarly institute, Ancestral Heritage, devoted to the study of the Aryan race's
origins, material traces and intellectual traditions. In fact, this organization is presented on your letter-head as a patron. Wouldn't it be
appropriate to ask along a specialist from its ranks, especially given the
broad public interest in the early history of the Aryans, their possible
contacts with spiritually and technically advanced peoples hidden
within or beyond the Himalayas? Shambhala is on the minds of people
these days.

Since you are so curious about this, I'll tell you that, yes, I did interview some promising men from Ancestral Heritage, but their age and
general condition were against them. This will be a journey too strenuous and emotionally demanding for anyone not young and entirely fit.
Anyway, we can only do so much, and I want to keep the attention of the
team sharply focused on our immediate goals, which have to do with
geomagnetic mapping, Tibet's flora and fauna, physical anthropology,
and so on.

But doesn't science itself point to the central Asian steppes as the
homeland of the Aryans? The study of the pre-historic and historical
record suggests—does it not?—that, before the beginning of their great
migrations south into India and westward into Europe, the Aryans
acquired their arts and acuity and noble bearing from a high, pure
source deeper still in Asia.

You have obviously read more of the literature on this subject than
I have. No credible observer has given us evidence that such a place
exists, though—you are right—rumours do persist in scientific circles,
and among aficionados of science. It is surely possible that there is or
was in the vastness of Asia an undocumented kingdom that has given
rise to the legends of Shambhala.

If so—

If so, these superior men, or the Aryans themselves, may have left
physical evidence in the cranial and skeletal dimensions of the latter-
day Tibetans whom Herr Beger, our field anthropologist, will measure
—traces of nobility glinting like silver in ore, despite the admixture of
Mongolian and Chinese blood, and the corrosion of Tibet's root-race by

centuries of Lamaism. In that sense, perhaps we will find Shambhala. We will gather scientific materials that may very well lead to richer understanding of Tibet's role in the primordial shaping of the Aryan race's project. But keep in mind that our mission is inspired, above all, by the Germanic thirst for pure knowledge, and by the highest German thought and intuition, such as that of the immortal Kant, who contended, in 1777, that Tibet was the refuge of early mankind during the last geological cataclysm that devastated the planet, and that the earth's plant species survived there — as in a nursery, Kant says — during this terrible time. Herder, too, placed humanity's origin in the mountains of Asia. Both men were thinking of the source of their people and of all green things in the language they had inherited from the story-tellers of their Nordic race, so — while they knew nothing about evolution — their spiritual geography is right. The radiant dawn of the new epoch in which Aryan man will master everything inferior to him breaks over the world — must break over it — from the east, from the mountain fast-nesses and treeless steppes of central Asia.

~39

My brother wrote letters to me while he was in Lhasa.

By the time his train arrived at the new, drearily modernistic, hangar-like railway station south of the river, he and his little tour-group had travelled forty-four hours since boarding in Beijing. The oxygen supply in his carriage had not worked properly when the train crossed the high passes, so he was afflicted by nausea and the crucifying headaches of altitude sickness. The days in Lhasa were occupied entirely with sight-seeing supervised by a pert Chinese guide who explained everything loudly in mechanical, perfectly memorized English. The Super-8 hotel in which his group was billeted, he said, was nice. but his Australian room-mate insisted on watching Perry Mason episodes, dubbed in Chinese, on television in the evening, which was not nice, so he walked to the old town, and ate pizza. It was while eating pizza, in a Beijing Street karaoke bar, on the edge of ancient Lhasa, that he met Jules.

He was about sixteen, I guess, my brother wrote, but with these Tibetans you can't be sure. Only the really old ones look old. He came up to my table and, just like that, he asked me: Deutsch? Français? English? I said American. He was dressed like an American punk—street-thug running shoes, a camouflage T-shirt, shapeless sweat pants held up by a drawstring. I figured he was a beggar, but nobody was making a move to throw him out. Other kids were in the bar, eating pizza, some were drinking beer, but nobody seemed to care, so perhaps there was no age-limit for drinking. Then he said, in rough but intelligible English: You look like you could use a girl. I can get you one, Tibetan or Chinese, whatever you like. I said I wasn't interested. So you like boys? he said. No, I replied, I don't like boys. He said the Chinese soldiers sometimes liked boys, but mostly they liked the girls who had come to Lhasa from China. There are a lot of whorehouses out by the barracks, he said, but the best whores are in town, the Westerners seem to like the ones in town just fine. Everybody likes something. You must like something, too. I said: I would like you to go on along now, just go on along. So he did.

The next night, to avoid a fight with the Australian over the TV, I went back to Beijing Street, to the bar, which was full of Westerners and Tibetan kids, eating pizza and drinking beer and listening to a Chinese girl with bleached hair sing along to Barbra Streisand CDs. He was there. He drifted through the crowd, spotting Westerners for his business, which he did nonchalantly, indifferent to the police who came in quietly from time to time, looked at the drinkers meaningfully before disappearing back into the street. He said to me: Is there anything you'd like?

I would like to know your name, I said. Jules, he said. A tall man who said he was from France but spoke English, who liked me, called me that, he replied, and the tall man left, but I liked it, so I kept calling myself that until everyone was calling me that. So that is what I am: Jules.

There is something else I would like, I told Jules, then started to become emotional.

At this point in his first letter, my brother left behind his fairly straightforward narrative style and commenced a spillage of nouns and adjectives presumably meant to describe what he told Jules he would like, but largely devoid of cohesion. He went on about the dogs, scrawny and hungry ones, that he did not see in the tangled streets around the Jokhang temple, about the Regent with jug-handle ears and a simpleton's chin, who did not descend from the Potala Palace into the alleys of the market, about the cleanliness and neatness of the ascetics performing prostrations before the entrance of the Jokhang, pilgrims whom the old books he had read said would be dirty, bedraggled. He was upset, I gathered from his rambling catalogue, because nothing he saw corresponded to the depictions in those books by travellers and explorers. He said the old quarter in which the Jokhang stands was being bulldozed to make way for a concrete shopping mall and an underground parking garage, and all the monks had gone, taking the ancient wisdom with them.

After reading this part of the letter, I began to wonder if my brother were syphilitic, like Nietzsche. My grandmother told me that syphilis, like masturbation, produces nervous exhaustion, then incoherence, and, in the end, silence, which explains why old negroes seldom have anything to say, syphilis (but not masturbation) being pandemic among them. The disease is unknown in chaste white men. Lacking evidence that my brother was immoral, I had felt his derangement was precipitated by reading — but a doubt about its aetiology now lingered on the outskirts of my mind. He certainly looked as if he could be immoral, on the morning he came here to blackmail me. The youth Jules, obviously in cahoots with the bar's owner and probably the police, took my brother to be immoral, or Jules would not have tried to procure him for the prostitutes. Indeed, the very fact that he sought out a notorious bar casts a long shadow on his predilections and previous history, since it is known that the dog always returns to his vomit.

~40

Be that as it may, my brother, in his second letter, related an adventure in the old city that Jules had arranged for him. One evening long after dark, Jules led him down a dusty, narrow alley running south from Beijing Street, past the mosque and the yoghurt-sellers' lane, to the entrance of a decayed stone-block mansion that had once sheltered an aristocratic Tibetan household but, since the Chinese Communists came, was home to a score of families, each secreted in a former bedroom, dining hall or parlour. The doorway Jules wanted was on the upper level, up a flight of steps, off the veranda that ran around the dim courtyard. He pushed open the door without knocking — he was expected, exchanged a few words in a language that was not English with someone inside, then said to my brother: You must never tell anyone you were here, the Chinese must never know. He motioned to my brother to follow him through the doorway. The air in the small room was warm and close, perfumed by incense, and by the butter lamps that supplied the only illumination. Seated cross-legged on a mat, his head freshly shaved, dressed in a monk's dark crimson robe, was a muscular, compact Tibetan man perhaps a decade older than Jules.

During the conversation that then transpired — Jules translated — the monk said he was sometimes possessed by Pehar Gyalp, the spirit-protector of the Dalai Lama, which made him the true Tibetan State Oracle, the man who currently held this title in the government-in-exile, at Dharamsala, India, being an imposter. The Oracle's identity had to remain secret, of course. Were the Chinese to suspect he was a high seer, they would immediately arrest him. He wore his robe only during interviews, and he never attended religious ceremonies. Indeed, to most people in Lhasa, and to the authorities, he was merely the affable, happy-go-lucky young man who worked part-time as a bouncer at J.J.'s disco. The truth about his ecstasies, his familiarity with hidden mysteries, had been disclosed only to an intimate fraternity, of which Jules was a member — though, on certain very rare occasions, the Oracle revealed his identity to genuine seekers from the spiritually impoverished West, such as Jules had apparently decided my brother in fact was.

When, at the end of the interview, Jules nudged my brother and said that the Oracle expected a sizeable donation in American dollars, and that he, Jules, thought he had earned a considerable finder's fee, my brother gladly spread the bills on the floor in front of the Oracle, and paid Jules what he demanded. He was pleased by what he had heard, and especially by the way it made him feel, the way all religion makes the deluded devotee feel — initiated, content with himself, grounded in the midst of a disoriented world, satisfied to be a sunflower bending mindlessly in whatever direction the prettiest light and coziest warmth come from. He was certain that he sat opposite a member of the Great White Brotherhood, which Madame Blavatsky said had persisted in Tibet, for example, when the Oracle assured my brother that upon his race, the Fifth or Aryan root-race, had been laid the mantle of greatness by the high intelligences of Shambhala before the spiritually and intellectually alert Aryans began their migrations across and beyond the steppes of central Asia. It's all in *The Secret Doctrine,* my brother inwardly rejoiced, misremembering Blavatsky's book, but immensely enjoying the confirmation of what he imagined the book said. And this confirmation was to be treasured above gold, because it came from a real Tibetan initiate, someone infinitely closer than any Westerner could be to the oriental source of deep Western wisdom.

From their redoubt behind the tallest Asian mountains, the Oracle told my brother, the adepts resident in Shambhala, survivors of Atlantis, had imprinted on the racial consciousness of the steppe-dwelling

Aryans certain images of primordial identity that they would never forget. They would remember the formidable white stallion of Shambhala, symbol of mastery, purity, victory, and they would inscribe it on hillsides, on coins and pots, and in their artworks. They would remember the figure of the all-wise shepherd, mindful and compassionate protector of his flock, wielder of sword and spear in their defense, bearer of the staff needed for their guidance. The Aryans, throughout their history, would always worship the youthful, energetic, upright Shepherd or Leader of the people, and would venerate the Sword and Spear of war, and the Staff of discipline, all straight instruments crucial to the survival and well-being of the flock, the tribe, the nation, the race. The Aryans, the Oracle said, learned adoration and obedience in Shambhala, and they learned what to adore.

But there's more, he said. At Shambhala, the ancestors of the Aryans learned a visual language they would take with them everywhere. The adepts ordained them people of the Sun, so they revered the circle, and erected circular henges of stone and wood, and laid out troy towns, emblems of the Sun, once they had arrived in their new European homelands. They were people highly attuned to the sacred geometry of earth and sky, so they honoured the Cross, intersection of horizon and ecliptic, pointer to the cardinal directions, image of the eagle or shaman in flight, of the man with arms outstretched in a gesture of possession, welcome, exaltation at dawn. They remembered the sacred Mountain of Meru, the *axis mundi,* in the center of Shambhala, and, though they were natives of the Asian prairies, they built artificial mountains — tumuli, pyramids, high temple foundations — in the flat lands their wanderings took them to. They remembered the sacred Tree growing in the garden of Shambhala's king, they remembered it until they passed from the treeless steppes into the forests of central Europe, whereupon they raised menhirs and megalithic pillars and columns, memorials of the Tree, and they became worshippers of the Tree's manifestations — Donar's Oak, and Yggdrasil, the Ash that upholds the nine worlds, and is home to the eagle, the dragon, and the four mystic stags. At the foot of the Tree, as at the base of the human spine, is coiled the serpent of desire — not the sexual tempter portrayed in the legends of the perverted, repressed Jews and Christians, but the embodiment of hot earth-energy, *kundalini,* yearning upward for ecstatic union with the eagle-like mind.

The Oracle went on in this vein for some time, wrote my brother, who was obviously finding the excitement for which he had made the long trip to Tibet. The tour brochure he had requested from the Chinese authorities advertised a thrilling scenic journey aboard the world's highest railway, instructive visits to historic palaces, temples and monasteries in the loftiest place on earth, ample time to shop in Lhasa's picturesque, ancient market, evenings free for enjoying Lhasa's nightclubs and discos. For reasons incomprehensible to me, given his hatred of cities and his fascination by the high Himalayas, secret kingdoms, Aryan origins and so forth — perhaps he was afraid, having never left the South, despite his claim that he had seen negroes in the American mountains — my brother decided to join this tightly organized tour in Beijing. But thanks to Jules, he had for a moment transcended, or thought he had transcended, the Lhasa of concrete dormitory blocks and glassy new towers and shopping malls. Out of the bouncer's farrago of folklore and occult scrap, my brother drew a sense of destiny that his life had hitherto denied him. He found someone exotic to tell him his origins lay in a place before history, a place not yet defiled by the miscegenation and perversity and beastliness he witnessed in the Southern city where he lived. He had found Shambhala.

$\sim$**41**

Or thought he had. Shambhala did not and does not exist outside the fantasies of Theosophists, elderly hippies, gullible moderns such as my brother, and Aryan supremacists of an old-fashioned sort to which I do not belong. That the white race is superior to the negroes is entirely obvious on every page of cultural, political and economic history, so invoking comely fairy tales or the writings of the crazed (but very clever) Blavatsky woman to demonstrate the proposition's truth is quite unnecessary. In any case, occult traditions interest me chiefly, if at all, because they interested Jupp, who interests me. Nor need we drag in Shambhala to explain the persistence of certain symbols in the creative thought of Aryan peoples from the time of the migrations down to the present day. The symbols that appear in Jupp's drawings and sculptures and performances on occasion, or again and again — the white horse, the stag, the oak, the shepherd's staff, the cross — are there because the artist's imagination was deeply rooted in the soil of inner Germany, the source, *ab origine,* of whatever greatness among the nations that the Germans could lay claim to. Jupp made visible in melancholy, monumental art the soul of inner Germany, as did some poets and novelists and a few painters, as did the untaught negro women who kept alive the songs of the inner South after the military defeat of 1865. Like the inner South nowadays, inner Germany is almost forgotten, is recalled by few artists and story-tellers — though I have seen reproductions in books of works by certain German painters that appear to emerge from a dialogue with inner Germany. All such artworks, however, would be consigned to eternal oblivion if modernizing, rationalizing men, such as Jupp's biographer and numerous German critics, had their way.

So remember the evening in the spring of 1937 when Ingvild Fröhlingsdorf, in the living room of her flat in Kleve's old town, read Matthias Zimmermann's illustrated interview with Ernst Schäfer, who wanted to go to Tibet in search of bird-skins, seeds and Aryan traces, and whose tales unsettled Ingvild. Remember her temptation to envy, her hankering, disagreeable in a woman, to go somewhere inappropriate, to do a man's job of exploring and collecting, to join the Tibet expedition as an equal, which she surely was not. Remember that, while Ingvild read the article, her husband and Jupp talked in Michael's study, then sketched in silence the plants they had harvested earlier in the day. At least this is what both the man and the youth set out to do. Jupp kept at his rendering of blossoms and branches for a while, then, as he had been inclined lately, he began to sketch creatures he knew from nature or from books or the Wagner music-dramas or from the church before he ceased to go — swans, an elk wounded by a spear, stags, lone trees in empty fields, silhouettes of naked women, Christ crucified. These images, new for him, were no more spontaneous than his copies from Thomé. His swans looked like swans, Herr Fröhlingsdorf commented approvingly; his oak tree was correct; the limbs and other parts of Christ's corpse were well-proportioned, which suggested to Herr Fröhlingsdorf that Jupp had been attending carefully to his mother's holy cards and the crucifix above his parents' bed.

Perhaps too carefully, the teacher thought to himself. Jupp, whose clean, clear spirituality was coming along nicely, must not now be seduced by Christianity. But Herr Fröhlingsdorf had noted, with a certain pleasure, the recent shift in Jupp's attention away from strict botanical description, at which he was, in any case, merely competent, toward healthily Germanic topics illustrated in the library's art books, where the boy found Friedrich's oaks and mountains, Grünewald's crucifixions, Dürer's hare, white horse, nudes, knights. His taste was turning from fact to symbol, Herr Fröhlingsdorf observed, like that of everyone else in the new Germany. People at large, in 1937, were now as weary of empirical facticity as he had been in 1926, when his desiring had been galvanized for the first time by Ingvild and by the movement. To be sure, he had praised Jupp's laborious copies when first presented with them, and had encouraged Jupp to do more of them, since he had thought an emotionally immature youth was probably capable of nothing more rich in national feeling. During the months since they began walking together and talking, however, Jupp had, in Michael's view, matured and deepened, become more German in his inward parts. Jupp's drawing now showed hunger for emotionally charged. post-rational symbols that were like, but more complex than, the ones seething white-hot in fiery speeches and flashing into receptive minds from Party posters and tracts. So, thought Herr Fröhlingsdorf, Jupp must have them.

〜42

In his third and last letter from Lhasa, my brother said that Jules had disappeared. He did not turn up at the karaoke bar the night after the interview with the Oracle, or the night after that. Questioned, the stout Chinese bartender, who spoke a little English, said he did not know Jules, and then said that Jules always came and went as he pleased, so he, the bartender, knew nothing about him, which struck my brother as implausible, but he could not make the bartender understand the urgency of his need to contact Jules. He wanted to see the Oracle again, because he had ten questions to ask him. Not seeing Jules on the third night, and with his time in Lhasa running out, he went to J.J.'s, where he thought the Oracle might be working, but he was wrong, or perhaps he was too fat and old to get past the door of the fashionably youthful club. He tried to remember the location of the Oracle's house, but after wandering for an hour in the old city's turmoil of streets, he despaired and returned to the Super-8 Hotel in Duodi Road, and wrote this letter. It took three months to reach me. My grandmother's negro brought the letter into the library on a rainy November afternoon.

I skimmed over the paragraphs about the evening's ordeal, which hardly interested me, but my reading was slowed by my brother's reflection on his single session with the Oracle. Since that night, he said, he had seen messages written in Shambhala's secret language everywhere. Perhaps everyday events and circumstances and things are not merely the mute, quotidian raw material of parables. Perhaps reality itself is parabolic, and the only modes in which the real can wholly manifest itself are poetry, myth, parable. While the body of poems, myths and so on features important cultural artefacts that reflect our race's high ability, I would reply, it cannot be turned into the basis for a religion without a sacrifice of good judgement, common sense. But, if my brother's weak handshake is anything to go on, I doubt if he ever had good judgement. I did not hear from him again until after his return from Tibet,

But I dreamed about him. He is sometimes dressed as he was on the morning we met, in an old suit and tie, but occasionally he appears in the fisherman's vest and felt homburg that Jupp wore in public after his breakdown in 1956. In one dream, my brother stands in a busy bar furnished like my grandfather's library, where he becomes impossibly drunk and starts to undress a waitress, who does not object. Someone is with him in the bar, a white man whose age I cannot determine. The white man speaks to my brother, the waitress he is undressing vanishes, and the white man leads my brother into a dark corner of the bar or library, where he beats him. The scene with my brother, the waitress, and the white man repeats. In another dream, also in the bar or library, my brother, dressed in vest and homburg, holds the hand of a little boy, who seems to be leading him, as if he were blind. The little boy stops and watches something unspeakable. He drops my brother's hand. The white man takes my blind brother's hand and leads him into a dark corner, where he beats him. These dreams mean nothing.

The fisherman's vest and the homburg that surface in the dreams, however, are curious details, apparently caught in an updraft of consciousness and deposited in the dusty attic of my mind during encounters with a 1974 photograph of Jupp, so attired. He strides directly and boldly toward the camera, his broad workman's body upright, his bearing serious, but unrushed. Another photograph, from 1969, shows Jupp, dressed in vest and homburg, spotlit on the edge of a theatre's stage. He holds up at the ends of outstretched arms great platter-like cymbals, ready to clash. I have this beautiful photograph, its imagery — circles, cruciform figure, horse — rising from deep German time.

Were I to portray my own deep time, the imagery would be drawn from a small white room in the South. There would be a small white room in a white house that stood beside a flat, broad field white with cotton, and the old house would rise white and clean from a shady lawn between the fields, like the house in which I lived and studied before my brother returned from inner Asia, and I came to the Occidental Hotel. Or it would be a tall house with a porch in a small town nestled within the fields, and white men secure in their houses and on their land, believing in a philosophy of the kind Jupp had, but no religion, nothing like that, no machines apart from trucks and cotton gins smelling of machine oil, no cities with frayed edges where motels are, no motels, no memories of my father in a motel, memories of nothing other than the fields and the white houses on Sunday afternoons, and the violently red clay in gullies or on hillsides from which the topsoil had been washed away by storms that came in the night and twisted the house's timber skeleton, keeping me awake with terror of the wind. No artist, I write this text about Jupp and about the South, and Alexander reads it as I write.

The night before I left the house of my grandmother, a storm, possibly bringing with it tornados, blew up from the south-west, impending, threatening to batter and wrench the house. Sister was away in a city somewhere, reading aloud from her works for grateful audiences. I knew where my brother's body was, where I left it, in the park. A dream: My brother holds out his warm, gelid hand to me, I shake it and it explodes in my grip, spattering my new sweater. My brother, now without a hand, consoles me on the ruin of my sweater with what seems at first to be a story about my grandmother, scented by toilet water, but becomes one about my father, who smelled interesting to his son at the end of a hot day spent overseeing the negroes in the fields. Before he can finish the story, my brother is led by his remaining hand into a corner by a white man, of indeterminate age, who kills him.

Figure 6: A frame from the 16-millimetre film of the action *Eurasienstab (Eurasia Staff)*, performed by the German artist Joseph Beuys on a day in 1968 not known to me, at the Wide White Space Gallery, Antwerp. The artist's right foot was shod in a felt-wrapped iron shoe. He slowly moved around the room, smearing fat into the corners and occasionally squeezing handfulls of lard in the angle of his bent leg, between calf and thigh.

The "staff" mentioned in the title was a length of copper tubing twisted, at one end, into the shape of a crozier, or herdsman's implement. Most interpreters of the event assert that, in Beuys' material mythology, the staff was an integuement, umbilical cord, or bridge linking West (technocratic, bourgeois, rationalistic) and the East (presumably "spiritual," transcendental). But it was also a phallus, transmitting precious seminal fluid. Salvation, of both the self and humankind in general, lay in the sacramental impregnation of the moribund West by the attentive East, thus quickening into life the foetus of Eurasia, the holy empire and offspring. To figure forth this fertilizing event was the purpose of the action Eurasienstab: *an inauguration of this event, ever new, and as old as the infusion of the steppe-dwelling Aryans by the inspiriting living liquid of irrationality from deepest Asia.*

The völkisch *opinions that underlay Eurasianism, originally a Russian intuition, enjoyed a wide vogue among Russians and certain white supremicists and occultists in Europe during the late twentieth and early twenty-first centuries. The genius, the appeal to the millions, of this movement consisted in its mystical hatred of America and capitalism and cultural modernity, and, beyond all else, in its rejection of the deeply entrenched canons of bourgeois, Christian-derived morality. It refused to indulge the enfeebling passion of benevolence, the inclination to equity or pity. It affirmed hardness, manliness, the violence inherent in nature, which is also human nature.*

As he went about his business in the film of Eurasienstab, *daubing the white, pure walls of his gallery with sticky handfuls of white fat (the stuff of life, semen), Beuys seemed increasingly distraught, desperate. His eyes were filled with tears by the end. I watched the film from start to finish several times in the museum at Darmstadt, and I knew I could never hurt him, never say anything that might harm him or impede his mission to restore vigour to the ennervated, Americanized German race. By the year he made* Eurasienstab, *1968, he had emerged from his crisis of the 1950s, remembered what pleased him in Germany before the war and during it. He had remembered the radiant idea of Eurasia, one vast continent under the irresistible sway of visionaries who worshipped the earth and nature. From that day in Darmstadt, I knew I would always protect his memory, despite Sister, who said none of it was true. I knew she was his enemy, and mine, and I know it still. She will never find me here.*

A photograph of Joseph Beuys' assemblage called Terremoto, *1981, in the collection of the Solomon R. Guggenheim Museum, New York. It depicts an old-fashioned linotype machine adorned with an Italian flag wrapped in felt, and a copy of a revolutionary tract describing* Action Third Way, *an activist political strategy, beyond capitalism and socialism, that Beuys elaborated in the 1970s. According to the museum, the sculpture also features nine blackboards and a metal box containing fat and lead type. The occasion of the piece was a November, 1980, earthquake that devastated a town near Naples.*

"The installation," writes the German-American art historian Cornelia Lauf, "reiterates Beuys' public support of independence for

this region of Italy." The machine "was once used in the production of the newsletter of a leftist political party, Lotta Continua (The Fight Continues). Grease has been smeared on the keys of the machine, rendering them dysfunctional. A blackboard on the floor leans against a small oil drum, as if elemental lessons would suffice to educate people to the inequities of capitalism. More blackboards form an altar around the printing machine. They bear alchemical symbols and chalk drawings of skulls, which might represent the victims of the quake ..."

"One important element of the Third Way is an emphasis on ecology. Beuys alludes to this in Terremoto by opposing technology with organic substances, and printed texts with handwritten ones. He developed this further in the larger environmental installations dating from the last years of his career, which are among his most far-reaching works, enormous in scope, magnificent in their intention, and involving hundreds of participants. They center around a single theme: his call for a change in thinking that develops out of personal understanding rather than from technological advances."

"... enormous in scope, magnificent in their intention, and involving hundreds of participants ...": Beuys forgot nothing of his German boyhood and adolescence during his career after 1956, as pointed out insistently by his hostile biographer and his countless bourgeois critics. He remembered the torchlight, the massing of men's bodies behind banners and standards, the spiritual voltage in his loins, and he became a sculptor. Not a trafficker in bronze or marble, but in older stuff—fat and felt and alchemical symbols, and obsolete machines such as the linotype device in Terremoto. Then he chose to be a sculptor in the most primordial material of all, as close to us as our own fat and bone.

"Only on condition of a radical widening of definitions," he wrote in 1973, "will it be possible for art and activities related to art [to] provide evidence that art is now the only evolutionary-revolutionary power. Only art is capable of dismantling the repressive effects of a senile social system that continues to totter along the deathline: to dismantle in order to build 'A SOCIAL ORGANISM AS A WORK OF ART' ... EVERY HUMAN BEING IS AN ARTIST who—from his state *of freedom — the position of freedom that he experiences at first-hand — learns to determine the other positions of the TOTAL ART WORK OF THE FUTURE SOCIAL ORDER." (Emphasis in the original. Beuys'* statement published in English in Caroline Tisdall, Art into Society, Society into Art *[London: Institute of Contemporary Art, 1974, page 48].)*

Our future is the comitatus; the horde; the herd, the band of brothers fighting underneath the stainless banner. Manhood knows this to be true, rejects what is novel, effeminate, what is untrue to the blood. The inner South knows this to be true. In his 1862 essay, Southern Civilization; or, the Norman in America, *J. Quitman Moore wrote of the everlasting conflict between "society" and the horde, innovation and tradition, "civilization" and nature, America and the South, the bloodless Puritan and the Cavalier nurtured by the Old South — the Cavalier: "the builder, the social architect, the institutionalist, the conservator — the advocate of rational liberty and the supporter of authority, as against the licentiousness and morbid impulse of unregulated passion and unenlightened sentiment. No idealist, enthusiast or speculative system-builder, upheaving ancient landmarks and overthrowing venerable monuments; but a realist, a practical and enlightened utilitarian, bowing to the authority of experience and acknowledging the supremacy of ideas, forms and institutions that had received the hallowing sanction of time.*

"An institutor by genius and a ruler by race, his pride was at once the sword of his most eminent virtues and greatest weaknesses, while honour was the touchstone of his character. Chivalrous in sentiment and magnanimous in deed, glory was his ambition, and loyalty the inspirer of his every thought, impulse and action. Elevated in his ideas and tolerant in his views, his selfishness was vicarious and his very faults wore the semblance of virtue. Unyielding in his principles, but compromising in his opinions, his conduct was governed more by sentiment than reflection, and more by association than either. Courtly in his manners and splendid in his tastes, a knightly generosity he practiced even toward his foes, and never lost his faculties in voluptuousness."

In his preference for obsolete technologies, antique materials, the values of the warrior band, the "social sculptor" — like the racist, like the

Southerner—manifests the archaism that has been endemic within modern art and modernist culture since the birth of modernity itself. But this phenomenon is by no means restricted to artists or Southerners. Start looking for it in the present era, and you will discover the long staring backward everywhere. This gazing into the distance is a defining disposition of the age, though the age, whose mind has been withered by various Enlightenment progressivisms, has yet to acknowledge its keening. The transcended past is regarded constantly, obsessively—at times with ineffectual affection (camp), at times with hunger for more vivid sensuous life (primitivism in all its varieties), or with desperate nostalgia for lost frankness, simplicity, probity (fundamentalisms of all sorts, especially the hateful Christian versions), or with pathological yearning for the certainties of childhood—or, in cases that are shamefully rare, with yearning for the truth of tribe, race, blood-brotherhood.

"Even in its degraded state, the dominant Anglo-Celtic ethnic core of Dixie and our Southern tradition still exists," states the contemporary white supremacist Hunter Wallace in a text he calls "Blood and Soil: How Southerners Became A Separate and Distinct People," where my writing is quoted approvingly. "It's the ethnic and cultural glue that holds together these contiguous states as 'the South'. If that ethnic core which was built up over three centuries is allowed to be displaced or its historical sense of solidarity is allowed to disintegrate, 'the South' will lose its coherence and wither away. We will become strangers in our own land."

∽43

In his understanding of the matter, Mr. Steinway told Alexander and me, the family wealth that enabled the owner to buy the old Occidental property came from success in real estate. Just before the First World War, the owner's father gambled all he could beg or borrow on infertile farmland in the foothills of the mountains near the city, then developed his property as a residential park, dotted with luxurious country estates for the urban *nouveaux-riches* of the 1920s. He had sold off all of them, for very high prices, before the financial crisis of 1929. Some residents persisted in living at their estates throughout the Depression, though most of them could no longer afford servants. An affluent one built cottages and workshops on his land for destitute artists and their families, thereby founding one of those last-chance places that came to be called "colonies." Alexander said that he was descended, at a distance of three generations, from two of the artists, both Marxist painters, who had sought shelter there during the Depression. They stayed on until the beginning of the Cold War, when prosperity returned to those Americans who, like the artists, were white and adaptable. The painters became abstractionists, and were popular.

44

But how, Alexander wondered, did the owner's father obtain the money to buy the barren land in the first place? Alexander is a curious child.

Mr. Steinway said that, before migrating from Naples to the city in the New World, the owner's grandfather was trained as a typesetter, quickly mastering the art of setting up the bits of type in frames ready for the printer. Upon his arrival in America, his craft was soon made obsolete by the linotype machine. But this technology, too, he mastered in short order, labouring in a shop that printed the Italian leftist pamphlet series called *Libreria Sociologica*.

For a time, the young man relished the company of the gleaming, vociferous anarchists who crowded into the printing shop on Sunday afternoons to drink espresso and talk politics. They were, like him, immigrants on the young side of 30. They spoke Italian rapidly and their eyes were dark. He especially liked the newly-breasted feminist writers among the radicals. and gladly typeset their atheistic anti-capitalist tracts throughout the period he served as an informer for the Pinkerton National Detective Agency.

For his work as a spy, he was well-rewarded financially. And after the proprietor of the printing shop was arrested for subversion and sent away for a long jail term, the police contrived to have him take over the business. He rapidly converted it from a small affair specializing in anarchist literature into a publishing house for a hugely popular English-language gossip magazine. The switch enabled him to build a printing plant, and made him comfortably well-off. He wore diamond rings and a velvet overcoat, but he had enough money left over to invest in his son's real-estate scheme.

Mr. Steinway said he did not know if the story about the owner's grandfather were true. But he did know that, during its Cold War heyday, the Occidental created and distributed to all guests, each week, a newsletter printed at the grandfather's plant in the city. Mr. Steinway had stacked copies of each edition in a corner of his office, and he made them available to the young woman who was writing a book about dead and dying resorts.

The newsletter contained stories about the guests' careers in the city, about their children, and about all the vital events between birth and death, though death itself was never mentioned. It featured the schedule of entertainment in the Tamarack Dining Room and of the rumba lessons taught daily by Donny and Louise, the hotel's dance demonstrators at the time of the missile crisis, and it offered an annotated list of the celebrities who were staying at the Occidental. For years, the publisher, editor and chief writer was an effeminate former busboy named Claude, who was transferred into the job after he told Mr. Steinway that he had once worked as a reporter in the city, and knew the newspaper business inside out.

45

Each Sunday during the Cold War, Mr. Steinway said, Claude put together the next edition of the newsletter, and, on Monday, dispatched the texts by express post to the city. There, typesetters using the 90-character keyboard of the linotype machine — young, healthy Italian-Americans they were, no longer anarchists or radicals of any kind — transformed the texts into metal slugs. The newsletter was then printed, hundreds of copies of it, on the concern's massive presses and shipped back to the hotel in time for distribution to guests arriving on Friday evening.

Alexander and I imagined a linotype device that choked and stopped when an attempt was made to enter certain texts on its keyboard, such as the twitteringly trivial ones Claude assembled every week, or the tittle-tattle and lies conjured up by the copywriters of the gossip magazine. But we know that innocent machines did not and could not exist.

The gin my father owned was not innocent. It clawed seeds from the cotton fibres, thereby reproducing its law, which was nature. The turbines inside the hotel powered the stage lights and loudspeakers in the Tamarack Dining Room, where soothing sounds and sights enveloped everyone, occluding every image that was not pleasant and peaceful, and, above all, not romantic. Romance, not only efficiency, was decreed by the machines. The linotype device in the city created information that was only about itself, about the perfected world of rational production it embodied, which was also the world and law and romance of the Occidental Hotel.

If I believe that machines can will, can intend, can even determine an outcome merely by being machines, I do so because they seem to know everything before I am able to think it. What they knew was harm: the discharge of a bullet at a coyote before I could stop Essie from pulling the trigger, the weekly eruption of hotel newsletters that reinforced the fiction of this place as the best imaginable location, the deliberate, hurtling advance of the automobile that ran down and killed my father on a road in Oklahoma and I could not stop it. What the machines knew was what they were, what they are. They are not weapons in the war of everyone against everyone else, they are the wills that refuse to let it stop, or they are nature.

Mr. Steinway remembered that Claude, editor of the newsletter, who had become increasingly autonomous with the passage of seasons, took charge admirably on the eve of the Cuban missile crisis. No matter what happened, he vowed, he would write and run a memoir of the visit of then-Senator John F. Kennedy to the hotel, which visit Claude recalled vividly due to the large size of the politician's tips to staff to keep quiet about his indiscretions. Nothing untoward or unflattering would appear in Claude's memoir, of course, and the future president's stay at the Occidental would be presented as an apparition of American goodness, delighting the children who crowded around him in the lobby, charming even women who were not Democrats. Already, Senator Kennedy had the qualities Americans deemed necessary in a leader of the free world — celebrity, street-wise aggressiveness behind a façade of nouveau-riche aristocracy, the insistent aroma of shanty-Irish sexuality: Such, *mutatis mutandi,* was the message about their captain that Claude wanted to convey to guests in the nation's hour of crisis. They must be assured that nothing had changed, that nothing would change, even were a nuclear catastrophe to take place.

Mr. Steinway decreed that Rudolph Sandman, who was in residence that autumn, was to be taken her breakfast of black tea, cheese and Ryvita at exactly 0900 hours each day, as usual. The adulterous liaison of Harrison, the Occidental's hulking lifeguard and swimming instructor, and Mrs. Mercer, well-known in the city for her activism on behalf of the United Daughters of the Confederacy and the First Baptist Church, should not be exposed. Neil Sedaka's performances in the Tamarack Dining Room were to go on as scheduled, and longer than scheduled, if the emergency lasted past the end of the booking. The turbines deep inside the hotel were to continue to spin out electricity for the guests' shavers, hair curlers and bedside reading lamps. Mr. Steinway prudently arranged with merchants in nearby towns to supply staples on longer terms of credit than usual in the event of the banking system's collapse.

The hotel's status as a whites-only establishment would be preserved, even if negroes were among the refugees seeking shelter after the city was destroyed. At Mr. Steinway's urging, Donny and Louise (who had balked) agreed to carry on with daily rumba lessons in any event, and Carl, the nervous elevator boy, was persuaded to keep smiling if tips became skimpy. Thus was the hotel prepared for the worst by Mr. Steinway, who was every inch an American, hence optimistic about his prospects.

46

He had been something else years before—not an American, not an optimist, but that was before the owner noticed him, working as major-domo at a certain risqué establishment in the city, and hired him as manager of the hotel in the mountains. Until then, Mr. Steinway had been shy but punctilious in his duties, which were menial and demanded vigilance. He flourished in his new position outside the city. As the Occidental Hotel became famous during the early years of the Cold War, so Mr. Steinway's stature grew, until being invited into his office for an after-show cognac was regarded as an initiation reserved for the hotel's most loyal guests. He was, in most other respects, democratic, even a popularizer. In concert with the owner, he wanted the Occidental to be a palace of pleasures and entertainments for ordinary, care-worn city folk. He wanted it to be a place of forgetting, a fountain (as he put it to Alexander and me in his usual grandiloquent fashion) of the waters of Lethe.

I write because I want to remember everything about the South my father came from, about American forgetfulness, about the cataclysm of modernity. The Occidental Hotel is huge. Even the travellers, a mighty throng, occupied only a fraction of it. Alexander says he has explored it all, but I do not believe him. Mr. Steinway says I can forget about my brother here, that the Olympic swimming pool is empty, that Sister will not find me here, that I can rest.

But I will not rest until I remember the night after the travelling folk, except Alexander, checked out of the hotel, and I was asleep under several blankets in the room with aqua wall-covering, and that night I dreamed of a man I had known in the city, around the time that I squatted on the riverside at midnight and did not follow the coyote. This jobless man lived in a condemned building at the forward edge of an expressway's advance. When he needed money for food, he strolled around the city, looking up. He looked at the tops of tall buildings until he saw a burnt-out warning light on a telecommunications mast. Then he located the building's manager and offered to climb up there for a hefty fee — the work was dangerous, and nobody, most days, could be found to do it — and change that light bulb.

The man had a remarkable knife. Its handle had been carved from a buck's antler, and the blade was long and very sharp. He told me he had killed someone with it, but I did not believe him, so I was not afraid. He said he used it for skinning rabbits, and I believed that, so I told him a story about listening to a dead rabbit behind the white house at Spring Ridge when I was a small boy, after my father was murdered. He said he used the knife for gutting catfish. I told him that Essie and I fished at the Blue Hole most afternoons during the summer my father was murdered, and the cook always gutted what we caught, then fried it up for supper. I lived with the man in his condemned building for a long while. On bad days, when the sorrow was on me, he sometimes showed me his remarkable knife and told me stories about it. We did nothing dishonourable. Then, one muddy night by the river, I saw the billboard advertising the Occidental Hotel, and knew I could live with him in a condemned building no longer. I thought I wanted the purity and clarity of the hotel, not the man who had the stench of a coyote about him. Now after seeking and finding the hotel, now that I am here, I know better.

In my dream, which I related to Alexander the next morning, the man with the knife was confused with the man who killed my brother, in another dream. My brother was menacing me in the karaoke bar that was furnished in the style of my grandfather's library in the South, and the man with the knife was protecting me, saving me, when all this was taking place in the lobby of the Occidental Hotel, which was new now, fresh and clean outside and inside, as it had been during the Cold War.

Guests, up from the city and the suburbs to enjoy the fall foliage, ignored my brother's menacing me, since they could see nothing that was not (because violent or contentious) in the sunny newsletter Mr. Steinway and Claude prepared for them. The law of this newsletter was the law of the hotel, where nothing of this sort could happen. Yet it did happen, in my dream: The man who stank of coyote and who had a remarkable knife killed my brother in the white room near the turbines, and set me free.

⌒47

And what would I do then, I asked Alexander after telling him my dream — What would have happened, had the dream come true in time, freeing me from the other son of my father's loins?

Alexander replied: You would not be writing this, telling me your dream, you would not be here in the hotel. You would still read and write in the library of your grandfather's house, studying Jupp's words and works, writing other things, not this — things meant for publication, things of which your sister, being a Christian, disapproves.

Your brother would not have returned from inner Asia, so you would not have seen him again, and that means you would still be in your grandfather's house, not here, writing about an unseasonably warm evening in early 1956, in Düsseldorf's municipal district of Heerdt, where Götz, having climaxed, rolls off Ulrike Slomka's muscular body. Lying on his bony back, he watches her stand up and slip into a fuzzy pink robe and a pair of pink scuffs.

He says something funny and lewd to her. She snatches a pillow from the bed and slaps it down hard on his hairy belly. He laughs out loud, curls up his naked body as if preparing to fend off a second blow, which does not fall. He fumbles beside the bed for his cigarettes, finds them, lights one.

She asks him if he wants a drink. He says he does, then stretches out again on the bed. He sticks the cigarette between his lips, laces his